Spellbound

Sacrifice

Diana Marie DuBois

Published by Three Danes Publishing L.L.C.

THREE DANES
PUBLISHING

Cover art by Anya Kelleye
http://www.anyakelleye.com/
Photographer Jean Maureen Woodfin
Model Tionna Petramalo
Formatted by EmCat Designs
Edited by Maxine Horton Bringenberg
And Beth Lake

Spellbound Sacrifice

Diana Marie DuBois

Acknowledgments and thanks

~ Lisa Angel Miller, thanks for always being there for me. For helping me flush out an idea and for brainstorming on so many stories.

~ James, once again my one and only, you know I love you and you are the only Julian for me. Remember the driving force is boobs. P.S. Ashley darling, thanks for allowing me to claim him. LOL

~ To all my readers, for your continued support.

~And to Wendi from Ready, Set, Edit for always helping me with those pesky page numbers.

Thank you Melissa Champion Ledet for helping with my pain in the ass book.

To Stacie Rich. Thanks for all you do

Note to readers

This by far was the hardest story for me to write. My heart along with Rosie's broke with each word I typed. Tears have been shed by all. But in the end there was a heartfelt goodbye. I hope you enjoy Rosie and Athena's next adventure.

Glossary of Terms

~**Baron Samedi** – The loa of the dead.

~**Bread Pudding** (New Orleans Style) – Lightly spiced bread pudding, flavored with bourbon, bourbon sauce, and bourbon-soaked raisins.

~**Café Dumonde** – A famous landmark established in 1862 before the Civil War. Well known for its beignets and café au lait.

~**Cajun** – Descendants of the people of Nova Scotia who settled in Louisiana.

~**Cher** – Cajun word for "dear." Mostly used in Cajun Country as a term of affection.

~**Gris-gris** – A voodoo amulet originating in Africa, which is believed to protect the wearer from evil or can be considered a good luck charm. It can also be the physical objects that are used in spells (such as gris-gris bags, which are either made of material or leather, voodoo dolls, and other items used in a spell) and the verbal supplications that are made to invoke the magical properties of voodoo.

~**Indians (Mardi Gras Indians**) – African-American Carnival revelers who dress up for Mardi Gras in suits influenced by Native American ceremonial apparel.

~**Jackson Square** – A historic park in the French Quarter that houses the famous equestrian statue of Andrew Jackson.

~**Jambalaya** – Spicy dish always made with rice and combinations of seafood, chicken, turkey, sausage, peppers, and onions.

~**Jazz** – Swinging Louisiana music made popular by Louis "Satchmo" Armstrong and others.

~**Lagniappe** – A little something extra.

~**The Gates of Guinee** – The entrance to the voodoo underworld, which can be found through seven gates scattered through the city's French quarter.

~**Pass by** – To stop by.

~**Praline** – A sugary Creole candy, invented in New Orleans (not the same as the French culinary/confectionery term "praline" or "praliné"). The classic version is made with sugar, brown sugar, butter, vanilla, and pecans, and is a flat sugary pecan-filled disk.

There are also creamy pralines, chocolate pralines, maple pralines, etc.

~**St Louis Cemetery** – Saint Louis Cemetery is the name of three Roman Catholic cemeteries in New Orleans, Louisiana. Most of the graves are above-ground vaults constructed in the 18th and 19th centuries

~**Second Line** – A tradition in brass band parades in New Orleans, Louisiana.

~**St. Louis Cathedral** – The oldest continuously operating Catholic church in the United States.

~**Baron Samedi's personal Veve** – A crucifix form deciphering the location of the seven gates.

~**Voodoo** – Mysterious religion involving charms and spells that came to Louisiana via the Caribbean.

"Love is a willingness to sacrifice."

Michael Novak

Prologue

Rosie

After I'd been consumed with death and heartbreak once again, I returned home. The trip had been exhausting and miserable, not to mention long. As I lay staring up at the ceiling, memories played over and over in my head; Remi's death; my best friend Jahane being stabbed to death; the last words she'd spoken; then, the last breath she took. Every horrible thing that had happened I couldn't forget. Memories flooded through me about my friends dying at the hands of my arch enemy's mom, Yvette. The sacrifice of them being killed to gain my ancestors' powers was not one I wanted to accept, though I knew it had happened. I woke most nights as the visions of the knife sliding into my best friend's chest ransacked my nightmares.

Then to make things worse, after they were both dead Marie Laveau told me she'd bring only one person back, but she kept secret which it would be. I'd also had a dream of someone telling me they were my protector. Even though I tried to make sense of it all the memory faded more every day. Athena remained by my side even when my tears dried up and returned. Julian stayed by my side as well, even though I knew he had many thoughts robbing his brain.

Julian lay beside me, his arm draped over my body. He hadn't really let me out of his sight since we'd returned. I was being suffocated, but I couldn't blame him...he was terrified of losing me. At night when we slept, anytime I moved he tugged me closer to him...a reaction I'd come to count on, but one causing me to place spells on him to get some space. I still needed my time to think.

No longer able to stay in bed, I scooted out from under his grip and said the usual spell to let Julian stay asleep.

Once awakened from a sleep.
Need once again to slumber deep.
Thoughts to ease and rest to reap.
Powers above make doze with a sweep.

Afterward, I nudged Athena to follow. She opened one eye and yawned. *What's wrong, Mom?*

"I need some air."

She carefully jumped, making sure to not jostle the bed, and followed. Once downstairs, I paced back and forth in front of the fountain. As I grew tired, I slumped down on one of the cast iron benches, and sadness crept over me. "What am I going to do now?"

Athena came over and placed her head on my lap. She was my comfort, my solace, my Guardian. The last time I'd seen my friends played over and over in my head. I had done nothing but cry since returning home. Feelings of loss and loneliness replaced happiness and joy. My best friend and Remi were gone.

"Is this seat taken?"

I turned around at the familiar voice, and even as he stood there glowing I secretly wished he was someone else. His smile made me wish he'd found happiness with someone. The harsh reality of the last thing Marie had said came crashing down around me. It slammed into me like a brick wall.

Remi was the one she'd brought back; his ghostly figure shimmered in and out. Suddenly tears streamed down my cheeks, landing on my folded hands in my lap. "Oh, she chose to not bring back Jahane. And you...you...are a ghost; you are different." I sniffed. "Why...?" My voice trailed off. I looked over to Remi and saw the sadness displayed on his face. "Oh, Remi, I'm sorry. How thoughtless of me."

He went to lay his hand on mine but it went through me. "Rosie, I know you wish Jahane was here instead of me."

I shook my head. "No, I wish you were both here. I wish we weren't in this situation. I wish lots of things." As Remi sat beside me I desperately desired to see my best friend one last time. I needed that.

He placed his hand on my shoulder, and I actually felt his touch. "Always remember Jahane loved you like a sister."

I sniffed. "I know." Memories of the first time I met her flowed through my thoughts. "You know Remi, the first time I met her she was so bossy I almost didn't think we'd get along. I remember we made pralines together."

He laughed. "She had a way about her, didn't she?"

I nodded. "The first day she came into the store she pretty much pushed her way into my life. Something I'm glad of now."

"I know you are. She was your protector, before Athena."

At the mention of her name the dog padded over to him and plopped down on her hindquarters.

"Take care of Rosie."

She lifted her paw and carefully placed it on his knee, balancing it on his incorporeal form. *I will, it's what I was bred for.*

"Wait, wait...you two can talk to each other?"

"Of course. I'm no longer of this world, so the magic in your dog helps me speak to her." He winked at Athena. "Your Guardian here can speak to the dead."

4

Only those I find worthy though, Mom, she added in a snarky tone.

Remi and I laughed. "She hasn't changed, has she?"

I never will. She stood and pranced around.

"So Remi, since you're technically dead, would you like a funeral or anything?"

He shook his head. "No, I've already talked to the witches in your coven. They've brought my body back and buried me. Since I'm a ghost and have another destiny, no need to mourn me. This time is for Jahane. Mourn her, grieve for her, but most importantly live again. She would've wanted that." Remi glanced around as if he was distracted, but quickly turned to face me, his expression sad. "Rosie, I must go now."

I refocused my attention back to him and a bout of nervous laughter escaped my mouth. I remembered Athena calling him Hot Brown Love. I nodded and wiped the tears away from my face. "Will I see you again?"

He tilted my head back. "You can bet on it, baby girl."

He flickered like a bad connection, then I was alone. I sat petting Athena's head, wondering what to do next, but I couldn't think of anything except the loss of Jahane. I solemnly walked back up the steps and sat on a wicker chair on the balcony. As I sat overlooking the courtyard, my body was numb, as well as my thoughts. I missed Jahane so much, even Remi.

"Petal...," my mama's voice broke through the numbness, but I never glanced in her direction. "You must deal with this. You have a hard road ahead of you. I won't always be here; I must leave soon," her voice took on a begging tone.

I didn't answer, just wiped a tear that slid down my cheek. Athena sat with her head on my lap, never moving. I was tired of death, especially of those I cared about. First my father, then my mother, and now my friends.

I barely heard the door open as Julian walked out. Still, I sat and stared at the flowers surrounding the fountain below me. For a second I wondered how he'd awoken from my spell but quickly squashed the thought.

"How's she doing, Magnolia?"

I never heard my mama's response because I delved back deep into my thoughts. How in the hell was I going to go on without my best friend? I'd lost everything.

Not me, Mom. I'm still here. I didn't reply to Athena, just petted her head. *Mom, I know it hurts—loss always does—but you will survive.*

For an hour—at least it felt that way—I sat outside, not moving, not really thinking, just existing. I knew I needed to move on, but right now I needed my time to grieve. Could I do this without my best friend?

Julian's presence remained but he stayed quiet. Finally, he spoke. "Rosie, it's time to go back inside. How long have you been out here?" I didn't answer him as he scooped me up in his arms and my heart hurt so much. I didn't fight him when he picked me up, I just melted into his arms. As I leaned into him I started to cry again. "Let it out, you need to." I slumped into his arms and sobbed. He placed me on the bed and got in beside me, pressing my body against his. Before I drifted off to sleep, he patted the bed for Athena to join us. She snuggled between us as much as she could.

Chapter one

Rosie

My eyes popped open. I scooted up against the pillow and rubbed my face. How long had I been asleep? Moonlight peeked through a crack in the curtains. I scooted out of bed, careful not to disturb Julian. My feet pulled me over to the french doors leading out to my balcony. Sighing deeply, I held the curtains open with one hand. Quickly I slipped outside again with Athena in tow. With no idea of what time it was, I decided to contemplate things alone. I paced back and forth, not wanting to admit it, and before I could stop my mouth from saying what I didn't want it to, it betrayed me. I needed to give the bad news to her mother.

"Oh shit, Athena. Mrs. Kellete is going to be so upset."

Not at you, though; this isn't your fault.

"I know, but she's lost a daughter to magic. I wouldn't blame her if did she blame me."

I sighed deeply; what was I going to do? My life was in shambles. I had magic I had no idea how to use, my mother and Remi were ghosts, my father was dead, and now so was my best friend.

Athena bumped against my leg. *Mom...*

"I know, we need to get it done, better sooner than later." I looked up in the sky and at the stars twinkling against the city lights. A city that never slept. I climbed down the steps, still deep in thought, and meandered around for a while. Pacing around the courtyard absentmindedly, my fingertips grazed the petals of the flowers. Yawning, I continued to walk, my thoughts a jumbled mess in my head. Nothing really made sense.

Mom, you should get some more rest.

I nodded and went back towards the wooden steps. Athena bounced ahead of me up the wooden staircase leading to the apartment. When we entered, Julian stood in the entryway. His face wavered from anger to oh thank god where the hell have you been. Before I could explain, he wrapped his arms around me.

"Rosie, good God, you are going to be the death of me. I was so worried about you."

I pushed back from him. "No need to worry. Athena and I were outside. Besides, we were only gone for a few minutes." Athena immediately growled. "Now look, you hurt her feelings." I patted her head. "You know she doesn't like it if she feels you don't trust her to keep me safe."

He chuckled and patted her head. "No hard feelings, huh girl? I trust you."

She bumped past me. *Yeah, right he does, dumb fleabag,* my dog grumbled.

I laughed out loud. She hadn't called him that in forever. "Damn, Julian, you've got a lot of making up to do. She just called you a fleabag."

"A what?" He laughed.

"Yeah, that's her go-to name for you when you upset her." I laughed louder as Athena padded into the room, closing the door behind her.

"It looks as if I do, especially since I know for a fact that for what's left of tonight she will be hogging the bed." He grimaced.

I cocked a brow at him. "Yep, you might want to get comfy on the sofa for tonight."

He grabbed me and scooped me up. "Only if you share it with me." He dipped his head down and the kiss lit me on fire. Passion exuded from the touch of his lips, causing my body to tingle. When he pulled back I looked up at him. A warm tear slid down my face.

"What's wrong, ma cher?"

He nestled into a propped up pillow and I sat beside him. I dropped my head in my hands. "Jahane is not coming back."

His expression was grim. "I know, cher."

"How do you know?"

"Your mother told me before I brought you back inside the other night. She said you were visited by Remi as a ghost."

My sobs became stronger. "Yes. He came back different. Just like Marie pronounced, one would be gone forever and the other would be different."

At this revelation he pulled me closer, wrapping me up in his arms and comforting me. "Oh damn, I'm so sorry." He tried to comfort me by rubbing small circles on my back. "I'm here for you."

"I know," I sniffed, letting the tears fall. I sobbed uncontrollably for what seemed like hours. "Why her, Julian? Why would Marie do this to me?"

He held me tight. "I don't know, cher, but I'm sure she has a reason."

I pushed back the anger that was coming to the forefront of my emotions. My face burned as the tears cascaded down my cheeks. "But what reason would she have to let my friend die?"

"I don't know, but we will find out." He pulled me back towards him and I wiped my nose on his shirt. He laughed silently at my action. "Rosie, I'm not sure, but if I've learned anything from both our experiences, things happen for a reason. You should talk to her."

I shook my head. "I can't, not right now. I'm too angry." I leaned into him and the tears I thought were gone once again poured freely. The fact that I'd never see Jahane again broke my heart and my soul. I didn't think I could ever recover from this loss.

A voice sounded in my head, my mother's. *You will come out of this tragedy even stronger. And when the time is right you must talk to Marie; she didn't do this to hurt you.*

I shook my head against Julian's chest, sighed deeply, and finally, the exhaustion of today's knowledge hit me. Julian slid down on the sofa, taking me with him.

I placed myself in front of him and fused into his body. With his arms around me, his long brown hair over my shoulder, I drifted off to sleep.

I begrudgingly woke up the next morning, surprisingly in my own bed. I patted the side and didn't feel Julian. But the smells of breakfast wafted through the room, rousing my appetite.

Before I knew it my mood fell. The knowledge that I had to go and tell Jahane's mom her daughter was dead broke my heart. A dozen thoughts swarmed through my head...would she hate me? Would she blame me? I rolled over and stuffed the pillow over my head. "How am I going to do this?" I muttered aloud. Athena crawled over to me and slapped her paw over my back. "Ouch, Athena."

Sorry, Mom.

"It's okay."

Mom, everything will be okay. Jahane's mom will understand.

"I sure hope so," my voice was muffled by the pillow.

"Rise and shine, Sleeping Beauty," Julian said with a smile and a tray of food. Athena jumped up, almost knocking me off the bed, the moment of her being mad at him quickly forgotten. He eyed her, then tossed a piece of bacon her way. "Have you forgiven me?"

She snatched the bacon and gobbled it down, then turned to me. *Tell him I'll think about it.* She stretched and jumped off the bed, then sashayed out of the room.

I burst out laughing and turned to Julian. "She said she'll think about it."

"I don't know if I'll ever get used to the fact you can talk to your dog."

I looked up at him and bit into a crunchy piece of bacon. "You better get used to it, because we are in for a whirlwind ride with magic."

He placed the tray down in front of me and walked around the bed and sat down. "So, what's on the agenda today?"

I hung my head. "I need to go see Jahane's mom."

"Would you like me to go with you?"

I pondered an answer to his question but finally shook my head. "No, I need to do this on my own. But you could do something for me."

"Anything." He leaned down and kissed me on the nose.

"Could you please speak to Mr. Jacque, let him know, and see if he can have the restaurant opened for after her funeral?"

He nodded. "Yes, I can do that."

"Thank you."

"But eat first; you need your strength, and I know you haven't been eating well. I mean, look at you, you're all bones." He winked at me. "I mean, I do like a little meat on my girl's body."

I hugged my arms around my body and knew he was right. Quickly I popped another piece of bacon in my mouth, followed by a fork full of eggs. Before I drank my coffee, I held the mug to my nose, inhaling the sweet tobacco aroma of the chicory. After I chugged the now lukewarm coffee down, the taste of sweet and sour nuttiness filled my senses and calmed me, though I didn't know if it was actually the coffee or my powers releasing a calming effect on me. But nonetheless, I would take it since I had to do something extra hard today.

I looked up at Julian. "Thank you."

"For what?"

"For being you and for loving me."

He pressed his hand behind my head and pulled me closer, his emerald eyes staring into mine. I could see so much love in just one look from him. "I will do anything for you, and protect you. I live for you and only you. We are in this together."

"Don't forget Athena or she'll be mad at you."

He chuckled. "Never again will I make that mistake."

I wagged a finger at him. "Very wise indeed."

He pressed his lips to mine and spoke against them. "You better get dressed...we have plenty of things to get done today."

14

I frowned against his lips and pushed away. "Yes, we do."

He pulled back and stared at me. "Make sure Athena watches over you."

After I got dressed, I headed out the door. As my hand gripped the knob my cell phone rang. I looked at the number but didn't recognize it. "Hello."

"Is this Rosie?"

"Yes, it is." I wondered who was calling me.

"Do you know a guy named Derrick?"

"Oh shit." I groaned. "Yes."

"Well, can you come pick up your boyfriend?"

"He's not...oh, never mind. Where is he?"

The caller gave me the location and told me he was drunk. After hanging up, I sighed.

"Who was that?" Julian asked, wiping his hands on a towel.

"Blah blah, strip club. I need to go pick Derrick up, he's drunk."

He shook his head. "No, if he's drunk and at a strip club you aren't going. I'll go get him."

"Julian, it's okay."

He grabbed me by the shoulders. "You have enough to do...let me. Besides, if he's drunk it's not a good time; he may blame you. I can handle this."

"Are you sure?"

"Yes, but I'll go after I leave the Brackish Tavern, give him some time to cool off. Since he probably stayed there all night, maybe they'll let him sleep it off."

"Thank you."

I kissed Julian goodbye and grabbed Athena's leash. I found her lounging outside by the fountain. She lay sprawled on her belly, her back legs sticking out and her head on her paws. She was focusing on something or someone so I waited, not wanting to disturb whatever she was doing. I sat down on the bench beside the fountain and reminisced about a time when things weren't filled with death.

Athena came over to me and nudged me from my thoughts. *Where are we going today, Mom?*

I sighed deeply. "Like I said, we're going to Treme to speak to Jahane's mother."

It will be okay, Mom.

"I know...I hope so. Just hate to have to tell her that her daughter is gone." Athena leaned up against me, pressing her weight into my body. "Let's get this over with." I clipped the leash to her collar and we walked solemnly out of the shaded courtyard into the bright sunlight.

Chapter Two

Julian

Sadness and elation overtook me as I knew Rosie's heart was broken, but she trusted me enough to help her in this time. I was going to have to pick something up for her. I watched her head out the door, shoved the dishes in the sink, and headed to the Brackish Tavern. Mr. Jacque was going to be devastated that Jahane was gone. I knew how much the man loved the two girls.

I stuffed my hands in my pockets and walked down the street. Once I got to the front door of the restaurant, I was stopped by a fuzzy apparition. Dammit, I was getting so used to this magic stuff. When the figure became solid in front of me, Remi stood there smiling.

"Hello, Julian."

"Remi man, I'm so sorry this happened to you."

He shrugged his shoulders. "No harm...just make sure you keep Rosie close to you. Evil is coming, and she'll need you even more with Jahane gone."

I brushed a hand through my hair and then shoved them both into my pockets. "Hey look...I'm sorry I treated you so shitty while you were alive."

He grinned wide. "No hard feelings, man. I'd have done the same thing had it been my girl."

"Yes, but still I was a dick in the beginning."

"Yes, you were."

I nodded. "Well, thank you for keeping an eye on Rosie when I did the worst thing ever by leaving her."

"It was my pleasure. But I must get going. I have a job to get to."

I laughed. "A job? But you are a ghost."

"Yeah, but we live in the most haunted city in the world, so I've got plenty of work to do." He grinned.

I eyed him. "I hope you aren't going to be trying to scare the tourists in the city."

He chuckled. "No, but that would be fun, wouldn't it? No, it's actually a legit job." His attention diverted to a tall blonde standing beside him who appeared out of nowhere.

"Come on, Remi, Drake is waiting." She smiled over at me.

"I'm coming, Esmerie." He made quick introductions, then shook my hand even though it wasn't really a shake. "Take care of our girl." He strode off with the blonde, both disappearing into nothing as they walked.

I turned, faced the door, and grabbed the handle. Hesitation filled me, and I gulped in some air. When the door opened, a gust of cool air hit me as I sauntered inside, where I was immediately greeted by Mr. Jacque.

"Hello. Where is Rosie?" he asked, his excitement causing his accent to become thicker.

I dropped my head, realizing I had to tell him the bad news. "Uh...Mr. Jacque, I'm afraid I have some devastating news to tell you."

His face faltered and his jovial smile disappeared. "What happened to Rosie?"

"Nothing happened...to her. It's, uh...Jahane." I didn't know how to tell him, so I just blurted it out. "Mr. Jacque, Jahane is dead."

He gasped. "How...?" His words came in incoherent syllables of Italian I couldn't understand.

"You may want to sit down." He gripped the table and slowly sat. After I'd finished telling him the gruesome story, he wiped away stray tears.

"This can't be happening. Julian, I've known those girls since they were little. Rosie must be devastated."

"I know, sir, and she is. But I have more bad news."

"More? There's more?"

I nodded my head. "I'm afraid Remi was also killed."

He looked as if I had just sucker punched him in the stomach. "What happened?"

"The same thing as Jahane. They were both caught in the same tragedy."

He hung his head. "Wow, Rosie. How is she taking all this?"

"Not well at all. She's having a tough time."

"Does Mrs. Olivia know yet?"

"Rosie and Athena are over at Jahane's mother's house telling her the bad news."

"Oh no." He hung his head, wiping away a few more stray tears.

"But I came for another reason." His head was still down and he sniffed, holding a handkerchief to his eyes. I waited, then continued. "Sir, I came to ask you a favor on behalf of Rosie."

"Anything...what can I do?"

"Can we have the restaurant closed for the family and friends after the funeral?"

He nodded. "Tell Rosie it would be my pleasure to help her in this time of need. I myself will cook Jahane's favorite dishes."

I stood and shook his hand. "Thank you, Mr. Jacque. Rosie will appreciate it."

I left the Brackish Tavern with a little—not much—weight lifted off my shoulders.

Chapter three

Rosie

As we walked down the paved sidewalks, I glanced at the rows and rows of shotgun houses lining the street, all in different colors with their tiny stoops. Once we got to Rampart Street, I looked across the street at the huge arched entrance to Louis Armstrong Park and decided to take a quick detour. The next leg of my journey would be difficult, so I needed to collect my thoughts on what to say to Mrs. Kellete. This was going to be so hard, the hardest thing I'd ever done, worse even than when I'd left Jahane and Julian.

Athena pulled on the leash so I unclipped it, hoping I wouldn't get into trouble. But if I did, I was sure a little magic could help. She ran off, barking at the ducks as I meandered down the path with low-hanging Spanish moss. When I found a bench, I sat and contemplated what I would tell my best friend's mother.

A hand touched my knee and I jumped back to stare into the face of Marie Laveau. "Oh my, I didn't mean to startle you, mon piti." Kindness was etched into her face.

I pulled away, my anger erupting over her decision. "What do you want?" I spat.

She cocked a brow at me. But before I could say another word, a strong wind blew and my mama interrupted me. "Why, Rosie Delacroix, that's no way to speak to Marie."

I gazed into the face of my mother. "But...." In an instant, I'd been dragged back in time as if I were a reprimanded child.

Marie placed a hand on my mother's arm. "It's okay, dear. I understand and feel her anger."

"Still not okay, especially not at her age," my mother replied.

I looked over at my mama, seeing her face filled with anger, then changing to sadness. Something was up, I knew it. "Mama, what's wrong?"

"Nothing. We can chat about that later. Now we have to discuss Jahane."

"What about it? She's dead."

Marie Laveau looked over at me with concern. "Rosie, would you like to know why I made the choice I did?"

I nodded my head and crossed my arms over my chest defiantly. "Sure, let's hear it."

She sighed. "Rosie...," she stopped, then continued. "With all the evil surrounding you, it was only a matter of time before Jahane would be caught in the crossfire. This was not supposed to have happened, but...," she shook her head, "it did. Besides, she was, let's say, a crutch for you."

"No; what she was, was my friend!"

She looked over at Athena, and her smile lit up her creole features. Her ebony skin glowed. "Besides, you have a Guardian now."

As she said those words, I remembered something from after Jahane had passed. It came flooding back to me like a sieve. *I was your first Guardian, now you have another.* "Marie, I remember something from after Jahane died."

"What?"

"A figure came to me and told me she was my first Guardian, and I had another now. Was that Jahane?"

She smiled. "Yes, it was. We've been watching over you all your life."

"How? I just recently told her I was a witch."

"I know, mon piti, but we knew when you came here you would need a Guardian or a best friend. Magical forces pushed Jahane into the shop that fateful day."

"Wait, what?"

She smiled. "Don't worry...her becoming your friend was her decision. We just pushed her towards the shop. She loved you like a sister."

"But...but...."

Then at that instant I knew what Marie had revealed was the truth. I struggled with this realization, though. Jahane would have always been in danger around me. She was human after all, unlike Athena and Julian. She was in a better place. Her job had been completed. I knew my destiny now was with Athena and Julian. The three of us were a force to be reckoned with. I looked over and saw Marie Laveau smiling.

"You know, you are a smart young lady. You are as powerful as any I've seen."

I glanced over at my mama, who was also smiling at me. "You are, Rosie. You are a champion among the witches. One to protect the city from danger."

"Which brings me to my next thing," Marie Laveau said. "It's come to my attention that a new protector is coming to the city." She stopped. "Well, two actually, but they are linked together. If you ever need help with any kind of protection, you will have it not only from me but from gargoyles and the Beasts of Atonement MC."

"But aren't I strong enough to protect myself?"

"Yes, but they have other attributes. I hope they will be setting up some sort of police system here. They run by a strict code. So if you need them don't hesitate to call on them."

"Yes, ma'am," I replied.

"Now child, hurry off to speak to Jahane's mother. I promise she will understand...maybe not at first, but she will come to see through the pain. Along the way, you'll find those that will help you put on a beautiful jazz funeral. You will appease the spirits and in turn, they will protect your loved one."

I stood and Athena leaned into me. "Thanks."

"You are welcome. I'll never lead you astray, mon piti. But my decisions will also not be made lightly. As I do, you must as well learn how to make difficult choices."

I walked away but heard snippets of her conversation with my mama. "Maggie, not now...we will tell her later. She has things to do, to deal with."

Even though I wanted to turn around and see what they were talking about, I couldn't. It was like an unseen force pushed me to keep going. "Come on, Athena, let's get going."

Yes. She bounded ahead of me, sniffing every nook and cranny her nose came in contact with. I knew she was making sure our route was safe.

We came up to the house that I had visited so many times as a young girl. The shutters were painted a dark blue color, and the clapboards were painted a bright white. I climbed up the cement steps, and my hand shook as I knocked on the screen door. A sheen of sweat creased my forehead. Patiently I waited as the door opened a smidge. Then it opened wider.

"Well hello, Rosaleigh. How are you...?" But before she could get the whole sentence out she looked around for Jahane. "Where's Jahane?" Dread spilled into her question.

I wrung my hands, willing my mouth to open, but nothing came out. "She's...uh...."

Mrs. Kellete's face turned a shade of white. "Rosie, where is Jahane?"

"She's dead," I blurted out. I couldn't stop myself, the words just tumbled out and I slapped a hand over my mouth. Tears streamed down my face.

"She's what?" She held onto the doorframe for support as I caught her arm. She wavered, her knees almost hitting the ground.

I looked into her face. It filled with anger and a mixture of sadness. She braced herself between the door and the screen.

"I'm so sorry. I didn't mean for this to happen."

Her eyes filled with tears, anger, and at least a dozen more emotions. The pain I'd put upon this woman came flooding into every fiber of my being. She slammed the door in my face, and her soft crying could be heard on the other side of the door.

I sat on the stoop and wept at the pain I'd caused everyone. *Mom*, Athena nudged me, *you didn't cause this.*

My heart pounded with the guilt invading my body. I looked down at my shaking hands. "I know, Athena, but if it wasn't for me Jahane would still be alive."

Don't think like that. She would have done anything for you, my faithful companion reminded me.

I shook my head. "Let's go. I doubt she wants to speak to me anymore. We should give her some time."

As I stood to leave, the door opened and Mrs. Kellette peeked around it. "Rosie, I'm sorry. Please come inside." She took my arm and brought me into the house, Athena following close behind. "Please, tell me what happened."

I gulped and sat down on the sofa. "Well...um...she came out to the bayou after I'd been kidnapped...." I hiccupped uncontrollably, letting the tears pour down my face. "Once I had been found I was reunited with my family and Jahane. My mother even returned, and it came to my attention we needed to find my parents' bodies. While we were out searching for them, Jahane was kidnapped to get back at me. They did a...," I stopped.

"Go on, sweetie."

"They killed her in a sacrifice to get my parents' and my powers." I began to sob hysterically. "I couldn't save her...I was too late. By the time I reached her she was dying." I hiccupped. "I'm so sorry. This is all my fault."

She patted me on the shoulder, tears falling down her face. "Dear, Jahane knew what she was getting into when she became your friend."

I looked at her, shocked. "What do you mean?"

She patted me on the leg. "Rosie, I know you and your mother are witches."

"You do? For how long?"

"Longer than Jahane. We chose not to tell her to keep her safe."

I dropped my head and muttered under my breath. "This is all my fault. I shouldn't have ever told her I was a witch."

"No, Jahane loved you like a sister. You couldn't have kept such a secret from her. It would have come out eventually. This is not your fault." She tilted my head up.

"But I feel like it is."

"Don't. It's evil's fault."

"What are we going to do without her?"

"We are going to live and carry on her memory like she'd want us to." She wiped a tear from my cheek.

"Are you upset with me?"

"Oh, darling, for what?"

"For harming Jahane, for putting her in danger."

She stood and walked away, but a few minutes later she came back with something. She sat beside me, and in her hand was a claim ticket. A sudden onslaught of memories came back. The day I'd come back home and we had gone to the jewelry store, we had both picked something up for each other. I touched the paper ticket as the woman I considered a second mom to me smiled.

"I think you should go and pick it up, don't you?"

I nodded, choking back tears. "I'd forgotten all about this."

She brushed a hand down my hair. "And no, I don't blame you for Jahane." She laughed softly. "You know as well as anyone that my daughter did her own thing. That girl was a stubborn one."

"But what if I'd insisted she not go with me?"

She eyed me. "How do you think that would have worked out?"

I laughed and sniffed. "Not well; she would have come anyway."

"Yes, she would. So to answer your question, I'm not mad. I'm sad and heartbroken to lose her, but Rosie, I know you are putting more guilt on yourself than you deserve."

I nodded. "Yes, ma'am."

"You need to stop...this is not your fault. Now, can you do me a favor?"

"Anything."

"We need to plan her funeral, and I can't do it by myself. I actually need to rest after hearing this news."

"Yes. What do you need?"

"Can you go and visit the Big Chief of the Mardi Gras Indians? Ask him to lead the second line."

"Where can I find him?"

"I'll write the address down for you."

"Thank you. And I think we need to find a jazz band as well."

A tear slid down her face. "You truly did know what my Jahane loved."

"Yes, she was my best friend."

She nodded and her expression grew tired. "Yes, come by and see me later."

"I will." I stood and hugged her goodbye, my heart breaking for her as well as me.

As we exited Athena stopped. *See, Mom, I told you. She wasn't mad, just heartbroken.*

"Yes, you did. Now we must be off to see an Indian chief." I unfolded the paper and read the address, and headed in the direction of the Big Chief.

Chapter four

Julian

As I left the restaurant, my mind was a mess. What else could I do to help Rosie? I had to speak to someone, and that someone was the one person I'd find in the graveyard. I headed in the direction of St Louis Cemetery. On the walk, I tried to keep my thoughts at bay. What would I say?

"What will you say indeed, Julian?" A familiar voice broke my thoughts.

I jumped. "Shit."

"Such language." She tsked at me.

"I just didn't expect you here." I waved my hands around.

"Yes, but you were coming to meet me at the cemetery, weren't you?" She eyed me.

"Yes." We walked in silence the rest of the way, especially since I didn't want to look foolish talking to myself as I walked down the street. The boneyard was uncommonly quiet today. I suspected Marie Laveau had something to do with that. She smiled as we headed toward the iron gates with the name of the cemetery above.

"Come, son."

I followed her through the maze of above ground tombs until she stopped. Not at hers, though. I wondered why we were at this particular tomb—in fact, we stood in front of a mausoleum—and then I saw it; the last name Delacroix etched into the marble at the top.

"Is this...?"

"Yes, it is."

"How come Rosie doesn't know of it?"

"Because it is for her mother and father when we find their bodies. Claudette and the other witches have had this ready for the day that Rosie could have some closure."

I ran a hand through my long brown hair. But before I could say anything, she interrupted me.

"I know why you wanted to speak to me, son."

"You do?"

She laughed softly. "I know everything that goes on in my city."

"So how do I help Rosie?"

"By helping her grieve for Jahane. Unfortunately, she will be grieving for her mother again. Magnolia cannot stay here forever. Baron Samedi will be taking her back soon."

"Dammit...how in the hell is she supposed to cope with so much death?" I didn't think about my language in front of Marie.

She ignored my brash words and continued. "Rosie, even though she doesn't know it, is stronger than she gives herself credit for. She will need to find the bodies of her parents so that their powers can be absorbed back into the earth and make her stronger to fight the evil that dares to corrupt my city."

"But...," I stopped.

She grinned at me. "Why can't I stop the evil that I created so long ago? Because I am no longer of this world. I can only guide." She looked away and for the first time, I saw the guilt the famous voodoo queen dealt with. "I am not sorry for what I did to Henri...I just wish he'd learned, as you did, to control it."

"Yes, but I have a duel supernatural ability, and he's just an evil man."

She ran her hand across my face. "That you do, Julian, and one of such humanity I never doubted for a minute you couldn't control it." She stopped and laughed. "That was until Rosie screwed up her spell. As for your ancestor, he was not always evil...he fell in love. Love will make you do crazy things. Your ancestor...he did what he did for love."

I laughed, then leaned against the mausoleum and contemplated my mission. "How do I accomplish this task?"

She laughed louder this time. "With Rosie herself, and Athena's help, of course."

"Ha, that dog has it out for me."

Her eyes lit up. "That she does. Guardians by nature are jealous animals and mixed with her innate magic, she is even more so. Besides, Julian, when she first met you, weren't you changing into a vile creature?" She cocked a brow at me.

I twirled the ring on my finger, the one I'd received from Marinette. "You are right."

"Give her some time still." Her lips turned up into a mischievous smile. "I think, though, that the dog is now playing with you. You and Athena must work together with Rosie. If you can, the three of you will be able to defeat your family, as well as Yvette and Gabby."

I let out a huge sigh. "So we didn't stop them after all?"

"Not all. Henri and Yvette, Dax and Gabby escaped. We found the bodies of all but Claude when we knew Rosie was safe and sound back in the city."

I pushed off the marble mausoleum and clapped my hands together. "I'll help Rosie and deal with my family and their evil cohorts."

"Good. I think Alma will be in the city soon to help, as will the other witches. You will need them if you and Rosie are able to find the bodies."

"Thanks, I'll be on the lookout for her."

"Watch out for your brother as well. I've got it on good authority he's skulking around the city."

"Oh great, that's all I need."

"Julian, shouldn't you be off to get Derrick?"

"Oh, shit...." She eyed me. "Sorry." I smiled. "I forgot. I'd better get going."

She laughed and nodded her head. I bid Marie goodbye and headed to get Derrick.

Chapter five

Rosie

I glanced up and down the street, checking the address until I found the correct one. "I think this is the one, Athena."

She sniffed in the air, then her nose went to the ground. *I agree, Mom.*

I walked up the stoop and stopped short. Athena nudged me and I braced myself on the door, but it was too late. The door swung open and a tall thin man stood there. He never had time to catch me because I was already on the ground. When I looked up at him, his smile was perfectly white, and his dark eyes showed kindness as he helped me up.

"Oh miss, I'm so sorry."

I stood up with his help and wiped my hands on my jeans. "It's okay. Are you Big Chief Mouton?"

"Yes'um."

I turned back over my shoulder and glared at Athena.

What, Mom?

I turned back to face the man and grinned. He waited patiently for me to speak. "Sir, I was asked to come here on behalf of Mrs. Kellette Olivia."

"How is she?" He bobbed his head and ushered me inside.

Athena pushed past me and sniffed him. *He's okay, Mom. But he does smell weird.*

I smiled up at the man. "Sorry, she's a little protective."

"In this time and day, you can't be too careful."

As I walked inside, Athena stepped between us. Big Chief Mouton sat down at a table containing a beautiful feather encrusted object. I brushed my fingers across the soft, vibrant red, blue, and yellow feathers. As Big Chief Mouton stared at me, I quickly pulled my fingers back, embarrassed.

"It's okay. You can touch it."

"It's just so beautiful. What is it?"

"It's a headpiece for a costume. It's almost done, and one of my best pieces, if I do say so."

"Oh my, it must take forever to make."

He nodded. "We take a year to build a new costume each year."

I gasped. "A year."

He laughed. "Miss...."

"Oh, excuse me. I'm sorry I didn't tell you my name. I'm Rosie Delacroix."

"I know who you are. Nice to meet you."

"Wait...how do you know who I am?"

"I also know you didn't come to talk about my costumes."

"No sir, I didn't."

Athena walked over to him, plopping her butt down in front of him. I shook my head. "Big Chief—"

He interrupted me. "You can call me Jim."

"Jim...Mrs. Olivia asked me to come by and ask if your gang could participate in her daughter's funeral." As the words flowed out a sudden pain tore at my heart.

He patted my shoulder. "She was your best friend, wasn't she?"

"Yes, how'd you know?"

He cocked a brow at me then slid his gaze up and down my body before answering me. "Remember, I know who you are. You are a...." He stopped. "The witch?" His tone changed from questioning to somber.

I tilted my head and looked back at him. "How do you know?"

"Here, sit." He pulled a chair out and waved me over.

I sat hesitantly. Again I asked, "How do you know I'm the witch, as you put it?"

He steepled his hands and grinned a mischievous grin at me. "First I'll answer your question about Jahane's burial. Yes, we will be more than honored. Second," he stopped for a millisecond, "you have been foretold to save the city of New Orleans. But there is so much more to say." He sniffed the air. "Evil is brewing in the city, and it's followed you from the bayou."

"How do you know all this?"

He leaned back in his chair; it rocked a little as the front legs lifted off the ground. "Let's just say I know," he said evasively.

I wanted to ask him more but I chose not to, afraid of offending him. Besides, I could ask Marie Laveau about this guy. She knew everyone in the city. I sighed and changed the subject. "I guess I should get going so you can get back to what you were doing."

He stood up and shook my hand. "It was nice to finally meet you," he said cryptically.

Once outside I stood in the middle of the sidewalk, wondering what the hell I'd just experienced. Athena bumped me. *Mom, he was okay, but as we left I had an odd sensation something was off.*

"What do you mean?"

Not sure. It wasn't evil, just something I hadn't sniffed before.

"Hmm. We will have to talk to Marie Laveau about this and see if she knows him."

Good idea, Mom.

I patted her on the head. "You ready to head home?"

Yes.

Chapter Six

Julian

After leaving Marie Laveau I meandered down the streets, headed to Bourbon to grab Derrick. The streets were filled with tourists, but not as many as they would have tonight. When I walked into the smoke-filled club, I saw him sitting by himself at a table, his head hung low. The bouncer walked over to me and followed my gaze. "Are you here to get him?"

"Yes, and I'm sorry for whatever trouble he caused."

"It's okay."

"Thanks, man. He's had a hard time...he found out his girlfriend died."

He eyed me and crossed his arms over his bulky chest. "Well, if he acts up again in here we'll call the cops next time."

"You didn't call them this time?"

"No. We thought we were going to have to, but Tara, one of our strippers, calmed him down."

"Where is she? I'd like to thank her."

"She's over there with your friend."

I shook his hand and walked over to Derrick. "Hey, you ready to go home?"

He turned to face me with a hate filled expression. "No! I'm going to stay here with Tara. She'll dance for me in my time of need."

"Oh, come on, baby, you should get some sleep," she cooed and shoved her big breasts in his face. Thank goodness Rosie was not here to witness this; she'd go all witchy on her.

"Come on, Derrick, let's get you showered and fed. We've got Jahane's funeral coming up."

He glowered at me. "Where's Rosie?" he said through clenched teeth.

"She'll be home later."

"Good, because it's her fault that my Jahane is dead."

"Now you know that's not true."

He stood, wobbled a bit, and inched close to my face. "Is so." His breath reeked of alcohol, and I almost vomited on the floor. "Julian, why are you taking up for that murderer?" He grew angrier. "Rosie is the cause for all of this," he spat.

I stood my ground. "Calm down."

"I will not calm down." He pulled pack his arm and threw a punch that barely missed me, but hit the wall behind me. He pulled back his hand from the broken plaster, then held it in the other and groaned. I was sure it was broken. "That bitc—"

I stopped him with a sucker punch to the face. As he wobbled back and forth, holding his jaw, I spoke. "I'm going to ignore the fact that you said that and blame it on the amount of alcohol you've fucking consumed," I growled, then I turned to Tara. "Hey, could you get a cup of coffee and some ice?" I winked.

She pressed her ebony breasts into my chest. One of the tassels that had been covering her nipple fell to the floor. She smiled, bent to pick it up, then grinned at me. "Sure thing, suga."

She flounced off, rocking her ass back and forth. I chuckled and turned back to Derrick, whose face was angered and red. He tried to throw another punch, but I grabbed his arm and held it behind his body. "Now dammit, you need to realize that this was not Rosie's fault. She is blaming herself enough for the both of you. She would be hurt if she knew you blamed her."

I let him go when his body slumped against mine. He dropped down into the booth and held his head in his hands. "I know, Julian. But shit, man, what in the hell am I going to do without her?"

"I don't know, but you will survive, as will Rosie. She needs all her friends, and so do you." I gripped his shoulder as I listened to him sob.

"Man, I was going to propose."

That's when I saw the black velvet box sitting on the table, the open top revealing a beautiful diamond. He must have been staring at it all night as he tried to wash the pain away with liquor.

Tara flounced back over with a steaming cup of coffee and some ice. This time she managed to have a little more clothes on, but her top still revealed her ample bosom. "Here ya go, suga."

"Thanks."

"No problem." She winked. "Take care of him." She turned on her heels, scooped up her purse, and left.

"Here, drink. We need to get you sober."

He picked up the paper cup and held it in his hands for a second before placing it to his lips. The cup shook as he began to sip. He put it back down on the table and picked up the bag of ice and held it to his bruised hand. "Thanks, man."

"No problem. Once you finish that coffee I'm going to make sure you get home to rest and sleep this off."

"Yes, Mom." He joked, but stopped and looked abashed.

"Derrick, she doesn't expect you to not live. It's okay to joke."

"I know, but dammit, I miss her."

"I know you do...we all do."

He stood, still a little wobbly, and stuffed the black velvet box into his pocket. "Let's get going. Jahane would kill me if she knew I was here. Besides, I smell funky."

I chuckled. "Hell, you smell like piss and alcohol."

He quirked a brow at me and managed a weak smile.

Once I'd made sure Derrick was home I ambled around the Quarter going nowhere in particular, my hands stuffed deep into my pockets. I knew I needed help...or did I? I was a witch as well, but had yet to unlock most of my powers. With all I'd uncovered about my past and my family in the last few months, a sane person would think they were going crazy. I checked my watch and saw the time. Shit, I need to get back home. Hopefully, Rosie was okay. I quickly sent her a text.

Heading home, cher. Hope your day went well. Love you

I waited patiently, leaning up against a building for her reply. After a couple of minutes, my phone buzzed in my hand.

It went as well as possible. Heading home soon. Love you too.

I stuffed the phone back in my pocket and headed off to the store, planning to cook for my woman. I figured she'd need it after her day.

Chapter Seven

Rosie

I unlocked the door to the apartment to see Julian in front of the stove. The record player played a sweet soulful jazz tune. I walked in quietly and watched him move his body in rhythmic movements to the song. Athena walked in after me but closed the door with a thud. Julian jumped and turned around.

I turned to glare at Athena. "Stop that."

What, Mom? I just closed the door.

I laughed as Julian strode over to me, grabbed me in his arms, and twirled me on the floor.

"Julian...."

He placed a fingertip to my lips. "Shh, don't say anything. Jahane wouldn't want you to be moping around."

I knew what he said was true, and honestly, I didn't think I had any more tears. "You are right." I let him twirl me around and through to the living room. When the song ended he dipped me and leaned down and kissed me. The passion that flowed through me sent tiny pulses to every nerve ending.

"So how's Derrick?"

He laughed against my mouth. "I'd be insulted by you asking me about another man while I kissed you if I didn't know better."

I raised one brow. "How is he?"

"He's hurting, but he will be fine." He picked me up and held me close to him. "I don't know what would happen to me if I lost you."

"You won't lose me."

He held me closer as we danced in the living room, but we were interrupted by a knock on the door and Athena growling. I pushed away from Julian to answer the door, with Athena and Julian following close behind.

When I opened the door I stared into a face I didn't recognize. From behind me, Julian spoke through gritted teeth. "Dax, what in the hell are you doing here?"

I turned to face him, then back to the guy standing in front of me. "Wait, what did you say? Dax? This is your brother? He's the one who helped Gabby, that bitch, and Remi kidnap me."

Before I could move both Julian and Athena had pushed me out of the way and lunged at him. Julian's fist connected with Dax's chin. His head swung back, and when he regained his composure he tried to speak but Julian interrupted him.

"What the fuck, brother? You were responsible for kidnapping my girlfriend. Do you know it's because of you and our fucked up family that Rosie lost two people she cared about?"

I'd never heard such language from him, but then I'd also never seen him so pissed.

Athena clenched her teeth around Dax's forearm. Her canines drew blood and it trickled down and onto the floor. He grew angry, but not as angry as I was at that moment. The hair on his arms grew thick.

"Don't you dare, Dax," a voice spoke from below us. But it was too late. I waved my hands in the air and threw him down the wooden staircase, where he looked up at Alma.

"You stay the hell away from me." My anger grew and the wind picked up. The water in the fountain shot up into the air.

"What the hell are you doing here?" Julian asked.

Dax stood up and brushed his hands on his pants. "I'm here with information." He walked halfway up the steps then stopped. Athena growled and stalked him, pushing him back down the steps, the hair along her spine standing straight.

"If you take one more step I will let the dog rip you to pieces," I spat.

Athena grinned, letting the saliva drip from her canines. *Mom, you give me the word.* She had grown more vicious with each movement Dax made.

"Dax, get out of here. We want nothing to do with you," Julian spoke up.

"I came to help you and Rosie."

"Help my ass...maybe to help that bastard of an ancestor find us," I said.

He grinned. "Damn brother, your girlfriend is a spitfire."

You haven't seen anything yet, Athena growled out, though only I could hear her.

"Shh," I tried to calm her. "Not now."

But Mom, he kidnapped you, with the help of that tattooed one.

"I know."

I glowered at Dax and noticed the uncanny resemblance between him and Julian. The man standing beside me had at least a foot on Dax; Julian's build was thinner—Dax looked as if he lived in the gym—but you could see it on their faces, except for the eyes. Dax's eyes were different colors, one a light blue and the other one a dark green. I couldn't stop staring.

Julian spoke first. "Dax, I don't want you to come back around here. You are not wanted."

"Fine, brother." Dax backed down the steps. Athena methodically followed until he was at the bottom.

"I'm not your brother."

Dax scoffed. "Saying it doesn't make it so."

Alma passed him and whispered something to him. The only thing I could make out was when he mouthed the word "Sorry" to her. As he trudged off I didn't care where he went as long as it was far away. We turned and headed back into the apartment.

Chapter eight

Julian

When Alma stepped into the apartment she grabbed me and hugged me tight. I pulled back. "Hello, Alma."

"How are you, Julian?"

"I'm good."

She turned to Rosie. "I'm so sorry about your friend. We will do a blessing for her at the funeral."

"Thanks, Alma." I watched as the two women hugged tightly. This was something Rosie needed, to know she had people on her side.

"So what brings you here, Alma?" I interrupted them.

"Never one to not get to the point." She winked. "Well, with the help of Alina we brought Jahane and Remi's bodies back to the city."

Rosie leaned into me, her body limp against mine. I wrapped an arm around her. "I'll be with you the whole time, cher."

She looked up at me, her eyes glassy as she held back the tears. "You are my lifeline, my brick wall to hold me up."

I kissed her. Pulling back, I sucked in air and let it out. "Always cher, always."

Alma interrupted us. "First thing we need to do is have a funeral for Jahane." She leaned in and whispered to Rosie. "I'll show you where Remi is buried, close to everyone you ever cared about. The other situation can wait for a little while longer, though not too long."

"What other situation?" Rosie asked.

"That is a discussion for when the others make it here." She walked over to the sofa and we followed.

I held on to Rosie. She was holding her own; she was a strong woman.

We sat across from Alma. "I know this is hard, but have you started making funeral plans?"

Rosie solemnly nodded. "Yes, I think we have everything planned."

"Then dear, why don't you rest while I speak to Julian?"

She nodded. "I am tired."

"Cher, why don't you go take a nap? I'll finish with dinner. It should be ready in about an hour."

I walked her to the bedroom and watched her scoot into the bed. Athena pushed past me and jumped onto the bed beside Rosie.

"I'll come wake you up when dinner is ready."

"Thank you."

I kissed her on the forehead. "I love you cher."

"I love you too."

I knew I had to take care of her, but I also knew she was stronger than she wanted to admit. I closed the door and headed back to Alma, who had made herself comfortable in the house. She stood by the stove with her hand on the teakettle. As soon as it started to whistle she whisked it off.

"Sit, Julian; we have much to talk about."

I sat and she shuffled over to me with a steaming mug of hot tea. "Here, drink."

After I took the offered mug, I watched the steam rise from the top. It swirled around into tiny designs I couldn't make out. I blew on the hot tea and the pictures took hold of the moisture in the air. I watched a scene play out before me, but none of it was clear. Alma watched me and I turned to her.

"What is this?"

"That, my dear boy, is one of your powers."

"What do you mean?"

"Well, you know you had visions or memories of the past."

I nodded. "Yes."

"You can also see the future in anything; water, smoke, steam, clouds, you name it. Unlike Rosie's powers, which are rooted in the earth's elements, yours are a mixture of nature and telepathy." She took a sip from her tea. "Though I have a feeling your telepathic powers come from your mother. You, my boy, have witch powers from both sides."

"But my dad wasn't a witch."

She laughed. "No, but you get it from me. I was born for a reason. To help you."

I looked through the tiny pictures dancing above my mug. "So what does this mean?"

"It means your witch nature is begging to come forth. You would have experienced this power sooner if it hadn't been for your rougaroux curse."

"Can I help Rosie with my power?"

She nodded. "But you must be careful and wise when using it."

"How?"

"When changing the future, you must be mindful of how much you will change it and weigh the consequences. Sometimes it's wise to let it be."

"But won't it be useful?"

"Yes, you can lead her in the direction she needs to be to fight."

"Fight who?"

"Henri, of course," she said with distaste.

"He's in the city?"

"I can't be certain. But I sense Yvette and Gabby are here. I fear that's why Dax is here. Speaking of Dax, I think he is really trying to help."

I shook my head. "You don't trust him, do you?"

She scoffed. "No I don't, but I think he's finally seeing he won't ever be close to Henri like he wants...no one is. Henri has no feelings or heart anymore. The anger has consumed him, it has taken a hold of his soul." She wiped away a tear that slid down her face.

I dropped my head and thought about what he must have been like before all this.

"Oh son, Henri was a good man before...," she stopped. "He was an honorable man, he loved his wife. We all have our crosses to bear and sometimes our families put unrealistic decisions on us. But like any man, he did what he did for love."

"How did you know what I was thinking?"

She quirked a brow at me. "I'm a witch remember...I can see your..."

Before she could finish I smelled something burning from the kitchen. "Shit, I let dinner burn."

"Julian!" she chastised me.

"Sorry, it's just I was trying to make sure Rosie had a good home cooked meal." I quickly ran to the oven and pulled the burned dinner out.

"I know, and she still can." She waved her hand over the dish and it no longer smelled or looked burned.

"Thanks."

"You are welcome. You should go wake Rosie."

I walked to the bedroom and opened the door. "Rosie, wake up."

Chapter nine

Rosie

I waited for Julian to close the door. Once he did I kicked the blanket off and dug around in my jewelry box for the matching claim ticket to Jahane's. Athena sat on the bed watching me.

What ya doing, Mom?

"Looking for something for Jahane." When I found it, I grabbed it and stuffed it into my purse with the other one belonging to Jahane. "We have one place to go. But we must be quiet so as not to worry Julian and Alma." I quietly opened the french doors to the balcony and we both slipped out. The sun was setting and a slight breeze blew around us. We were careful to not make a sound as we descended the steps. I quickened my pace as we headed through the courtyard. As we exited I held the cast iron gate, but when I let go it clanked against the hasp. "Damn," I muttered.

I stilled in my spot, holding my breath, and waited for Julian to run outside and see where the noise came from. When he didn't, I exhaled. "Come on, Athena, let's hurry before he notices we are gone."

Coming, Mom.

The walk to the jewelry store went quickly. I turned the corner and there in front of me was one of the last places I'd visited with Jahane. The store held probably the most priceless items belonging to my best friend and me.

Standing in front of the glass door, I inhaled then slowly exhaled before placing my hand on the knob. I stepped inside and instantly felt sick. I was supposed to do this with my best friend, not by myself, and certainly not to get something for her funeral.

Athena nudged me gently to continue. The bell above the door tingled as it shut behind me. I looked around and choked back a sob. I'd last been here with Jahane.

"How may I help you?" A young woman stepped out from behind the counter. Her high heels clacked against the floor. Her appearance screamed bohemian fashion, much the same as mine. The black bob that framed her face brought out a natural beauty since she didn't seem to have an ounce of makeup.

"I...um...." I dug my hand into my purse and grabbed the tickets. "I need to pick these up, please. Also, I hadn't paid for the engraving yet."

She smiled, glanced at the tickets, and picked them up. "Sure, just let me go get them from the back."

As I waited a calmness came over me. I had no idea where it came from. I looked over at Athena, wondering if she was doing it, but if she was she showed no sign. Instead, she was sniffing around the glass cases.

The lady came from the back with two velvet jewelry boxes. She placed them in a small brown bag with the jewelry store's logo stamped on it in a deep purple. "Here you go."

"Thank you." I took the bag by the handle and fumbled in my purse to pay for the engravings on both, but the woman touched my hand, stopping me.

"No need, it's already been paid for."

"By who?"

"Not sure." She held out the ticket and I recognized the familiar handwriting of my best friend.

"Thanks, ma'am." I grinned, knowing my best friend would always be with me. "Come on, Athena."

As I left I realized the woman never said a thing about my dog being in there.

She couldn't see me.

I stopped. "Do you have a new power?"

She bobbed her head up and down. *I think so. I just concentrated on not being there. I even nudged her once or twice and she never felt me.*

I laughed, a sound I didn't recognize since losing Jahane. "Let's get back home before Julian and Alma start worrying."

We scurried up the steps in silence. I peeked in the window and Julian and Alma were standing by the stove. "Hurry, Athena. We must get back to the room."

We tiptoed over and carefully I opened the door to my room. Sneaking inside, I kicked off my shoes and slid into the bed just as the door opened.

"Rosie, wake up."

I rolled over. "It smells good."

In two strides he stood in front of me. "I hope you're hungry."

"I'm famished."

The three of us sat at the table that Alma had miraculously set in the few minutes it took Julian to come get me. "Oh, Alma, the table looks so good. I haven't used it since Mama died."

"Well, it's a waste not to use it."

Julian pulled the chair out for me and I sat. Athena bounded over to her bowl, and I laughed as she waited for the food to be dropped into it.

"I didn't forget about you," Julian said as he dropped a few morsels of dinner into the metal bowl then petted her head. We ate dinner in silence, each pondering our own thoughts.

After dinner I excused myself. "Julian, I'll be right back."

"Do you need me?"

"No, I just need some alone time."

Athena stayed in the living room with Julian and Alma. I had yet to take a look at what I'd picked up from the jewelry store. I walked into my bedroom, grabbed the bag, and headed outside, where I positioned myself in the wooden rocking chair with the bag on my lap. My hands shook as they dipped into the bag. My trembling hands caused me to drop the box, but thankfully it didn't fall from the balcony. I bent down and scooped it up, and slowly opened the box.

Inside sat a beautiful silver and turquoise bracelet. I picked it up. "Damn, Jahane, I miss you." My hand shook a little as I flipped the bracelet over in my hand and read the inscription.

Shared Hearts, Shared Souls, Sisters Always.

A single tear fell from my eye and I looked up into the sky. "I miss you, Jahane. I miss you so much," I said as I held the beautiful memento from my best friend close to my chest.

I walked back inside with my bracelet wrapped around my wrist and the other one still in the box. "Julian, I need you to take me somewhere."

He turned to face me. "Where?"

"The funeral home." I grinned at his questioning expression.

"Uh, I think it's closed."

"I'm sure it is, but this is important. I have something to give to her, and I won't have time to give it tomorrow."

He stood. "Well, we need to pick someone else up. Do you have any idea of how we are going to get in?"

"If no one's there we will use our magic."

Chapter Ten

Julian

I laughed at how ballsy Rosie was getting. "Then let's get going."

Athena bounded ahead, followed by Rosie. She grabbed my hand and we walked in silence to my car. I figured it best if we got there as fast as we could. Rosie was quiet on the way. I wished I knew what thoughts plagued her, but I knew better than to push. After a while, I pulled up in front of Derrick's house. "Wait right here, I'll be back."

I jumped out of the car and made it to Derrick's door in a few strides. After I knocked on the door, I turned around to see Athena's head hanging out the driver's side window. I chuckled. "Damn dog."

"Hey, Julian."

I turned back around. "Derrick, you need to come with us, and bring that ring."

"Why?"

"Because you and Rosie need some closure and alone time with Jahane. We've got a plan."

"What kind of plan?"

"We'll explain in the car."

He looked around me. "How's she doing?"

"Better, but she misses you."

"Okay, let's go."

"Don't you need to get...?"

He patted his pocket with a well-bandaged hand. "Right here. I've been holding on to it since...well, you know."

I nodded. "Yeah man." I inclined my head to his hand. "Is it broken?"

"No, just badly bruised."

He followed me to the car and I opened the door. "Athena, move over," Rosie said as I opened the door.

I scooted in and Derrick got into the back, where Athena sprawled her body over him. Rosie faced the back seat and chuckled. "I guess she missed you."

"I guess so." I saw him smile weakly from the rearview mirror.

"Derrick...," she hesitated, "I'm so sorry."

"I know, Rosie." He smiled sadly at her.

"Cher, you ready?"

"Yes."

"Where are we going?" Derrick asked.

"Julian, you didn't tell him where we were going?"

"No, I didn't want to freak him out." I waggled my eyes and whispered to her. "Does he know all about the magic and witchy stuff?"

She shook her head. "Not everything. I mean, he was privy to some stuff, but I don't think he knows the full deal."

She settled into her seat and it got unbearably quiet. I took a right and there ahead of us stood the funeral home.

"Let's do this fast so we don't end up in the pokey."

Derrick laughed so loud I slammed on the brakes. "Where the hell did you learn the word pokey?" he asked me.

"I don't know, some TV game show or something." From the corner of my eye, I could see Rosie trying her damnedest not to laugh. "Go ahead and laugh, cher."

She shook her head, but couldn't hold it in much longer and burst into laughter. "Seriously, Julian; pokey?"

I winked at her. "I'm full of all kinds of interesting old facts."

"Yes, yes you are."

"Okay, let's get this done."

"How are we going to get in?" Derrick asked.

Rosie turned to him. "Why, with magic of course." Her eyes lit up, making her look like the old Rosie. She seemed to be trying to move on, though I didn't know how long this would last.

I pulled the car over and quietly got out, and Athena pranced ahead of us. "Don't worry, Julian, she's scoping the place out."

We followed, but the whole time I was on high alert. We got to the back door and Athena stood there with it wide open.

"How'd...? Never mind," Derrick said, astonished.

Rosie grinned. "Yeah, better to not ask." We all slipped inside, shutting the door as we did.

"What about the alarm?"

"Don't worry, Athena shut it off."

"What do you mean, Athena—?" Derrick began to ask.

"Don't worry about that. We have to find Jahane's body."

Derrick stopped in his tracks. "What the hell do you mean? We aren't going to bring...."

I walked up to him and placed my hand on his shoulder. "No, we are telling her goodbye."

"How?"

"Anyway you feel in your heart."

"How will we find her?"

"With Athena, of course," Rosie spoke up.

Chapter eleven

Rosie

We walked in silence down the hallway after hallway. Athena's nose was to the ground, searching and searching for her.
I found her, Mom.
"Good; where?"
She pointed with her head to a door to the right of us. *In there.*

I willed my feet to move but they wouldn't, so Athena opened the door and nudged me through. It swung open and I gasped a little too loudly. Before me stood a black shiny casket. We hadn't planned on a service before the funeral, so this was the only time I would be able to give her my gift. And something told me Derrick had something for her too.

I walked forward into the room, everything else gone from my mind. Julian lifted the lid very carefully. I willed myself not to cry, but it was so hard. This would be the last time I ever saw my best friend.

Once the lid was up I saw her beautiful serene face, her black curls framing her face. "Derrick, you go first."

He nodded, his face now red and streaked with tears, his hand stuffed deep into his pocket. As he went up to the casket I saw from the back that he took a small box out. I sat down in a chair by the wall and gave him time to tell her goodbye.

Athena sat beside me. *Mom, can I go next?*

"Sure you can."

We waited for some time while Derrick said his goodbyes. Finally, he came back over and sat down by me. I watched as Athena solemnly walked over to the casket and carefully put her front paws on the edge. I turned to Derrick beside me. "I'm so sorry. I had no idea you were going to propose."

"How'd you know?"

"A girl's intuition. Besides, you pulled a little black ring box out of your pocket."

He smiled weakly back at me. "You know I don't blame you."

"It's okay if you do...after all, I still blame myself."

He placed both his big hands on my shoulders and turned me to face him. "It's not your fault.

She would've followed you to the depths of hell if it meant protecting you."

A warm tear slid down my cheek. "Thank you for saying that."

Athena slid her head onto my lap. *Mom, your turn.*

I stood and ambled over to the box that would contain my friend forever. Once I was standing in front of it, a slew of tears fell. I whispered, "How am I going to go on?" I pulled the box from my purse to reveal a beautiful silver bracelet, but to my surprise, the inscription was not the one I had requested, but the same as the one she'd had put on mine. I slipped it over her wrist. On her finger was a beautiful diamond ring, and beside her was a small voodoo doll. It must have been from Athena...nothing surprised me about that dog anymore.

I patted Jahane's shoulder. "I'll miss you, my dear friend, my sister." I glanced over at Julian and nodded my head. He closed the lid and locked it. Afterward, I said a quick spell to protect her and the items we had placed inside.

Chapter twelve

Rosie

The next day

It had been seven days since Jahane died. Standing in front of the mirror, I stared back at my reflection, one I didn't recognize. I'd aged in the last few months. I smoothed down the black dress I wore and brushed a strand of hair away from my face.

From behind me, I sensed Julian standing in the doorway watching me. When I turned around a sad expression was etched on his face. He looked handsome in the suit, his red shirt highlighting the solemn look, and his hair was neatly tied back, showing off his square jawline.

I mustered up a smile, but my voice cracked. "Are you ready to go?"

"If you are."

"I have to be."

As I walked out of the room, Julian placed a hand on my lower back. The touch comforted me as he led me out into the living room, where Athena and Alma sat waiting for us. Athena was adorned with a black collar instead of her usual pink one. Her teardrop amulet dangled, but the color was dull. Athena's head drooped.

I sauntered over to her and knelt down. "Athena, I know you miss her."

I do, Mom. We all do.

"Where did you get the black collar?"

I picked it up one day when we first got back.

A smile creased my face and I hugged her head. "You are a good Guardian. But I don't like you out by yourself. What if the police find you without an owner?"

I'll just make myself invisible and freak them out, she snorted.

"I bet you will."

I stood and Julian grabbed me by the hand.

"Are you ready?" he asked.

I nodded but didn't speak.

We stepped outside and were greeted by at least a dozen people all dressed in black. Behind them stood a jazz band. They held their instruments ready to play at a second's notice. Alma walked past me, Julian, and Athena, and handed us handkerchiefs. Then she descended down the steps, passing the rest out for everyone else. A black umbrella laced with fringe at the bottom balanced on the balcony. Julian handed it to me. I held it in my hand and descended the wooden steps, and met Mrs. Kellette at the bottom.

She came over and hugged me tight. "It's beautiful. Jahane would've loved it." She wiped at a tear that slid down her cheek.

"Thank you." I nodded and smiled. "She really would've." As soon as I walked into the crowd it dispersed to reveal a gorgeous black casket laying on a flat carriage. I strolled over to the black iron gate and stopped. My hand shook and grasped the metal. Leaning against the wrought iron, I fought the urge to run back inside my house and curl into a ball in my bed. That coffin, it contained my friend. The horse neighed and pawed the ground.

I gasped. "I can't do this," I whispered. I sensed Julian and Athena both standing beside me.

Yes, you can, Athena whispered to me.

As I willed my body to move it betrayed me. After counting to ten, I sucked in a deep breath and walked over to the coffin, running my hands along the edge.

Athena followed me through the crowd. *Are you ready, Mom*?

I nodded, and Julian, Mrs. Kellette, and Derrick stood on either side of us. The others followed us, exiting the courtyard led by the jazz band and the Mardi Gras Indians, led by Big Chief Mouton. The melodic tunes of the horns sifted through the air and followed us down the street. We proceeded down Burgundy Street, then made our way with slow methodical steps to Basin Street, toward St. Louis Cemetery Number One, the same place Marie Laveau was buried. I knew she'd look over Jahane always.

The music behind us took on a somber tune. We trudged along, moving slowly with the music. As we headed down the street, I glanced up at the people in the balconies. I noticed something that was out of place...a gargoyle perched up on one of the buildings. We didn't have gargoyles in the city. But then I remembered Marie Laveau had said they were coming here.

I shook my head and continued walking. With every step, my heart broke. Athena walked close to me the whole way to the cemetery. I stopped just inches from the huge cast iron gate leading inside.

"Cher, you can do this."

"I can?" I asked, not sure if I could. After a second of hesitation, I pushed forward. We proceeded into the cemetery, the mausoleums all guarding us against the sun. Athena, Julian, and I led the procession, followed by Derrick and Jahane's mom. We strolled through with our handkerchiefs waved in the air.

The people behind me lined inside the cemetery as the music took on an upbeat tone. I held my umbrella over my head. We stopped in front of a huge marble mausoleum and Miss Alina stepped forward. "Before we let go of Jahane we would like to offer a blessing." Elspeth, Marron, even Madame Claudette stepped out of the crowd. A few others I didn't recognize joined them. They created a circle then began to chant in unison.

"Powers surround and hear our plea
Passing on now to let her spirit be free.
In our hearts, you are forever with thee.
Spirit rise to rest and blessed be."

Athena and I stood in the middle, my hand resting on the side of the marble. The tears flowed freely, sliding down my cheeks to my chin. Big Chief Mouton walked over to us.

"You ready, Rosie?"

"Yes."

He wore the headpiece I'd seen the other day on the table. The colors were vibrant under the midday sun. He danced and strutted and shook his body, then chanted as they placed the coffin inside the mausoleum. The rest of the procession continued to dance in a celebration of Jahane's life. I knew if she had been there she'd have enjoyed it, waving her handkerchief in the air.

Off in the distance, I saw a man leaning beside a tomb. His face resembled a skeleton and a black top hat sat upon his head. In his hand he held a staff dangling with tiny skulls.

Marie Laveau came to stand beside me. "Here, mon piti, take these," she said and handed me a bag of items.

"Who is that?" I asked as an invisible force pulled me forward to the man and away from the crowd.

"Someone who will allow you to say a final goodbye."

The mausoleum he stood in front of was run down, the roots of the trees holding it up and maybe together as well. Branches hugged the façade tightly. It was the only tomb with grass growing around it, almost ankle deep. Was I dreaming? It seemed like it didn't belong here. When I stood in front of him he blew smoke around me from the cigar in his mouth. The skulls shook on the staff even though it was still.

"Hello, Rosie Delacroix, I'm Baron Samedi. I am loa of the dead." He puffed again on the cigar, and when he removed it from his mouth, little skulls danced to and fro...some had umbrellas and some had instruments. Others danced in a morbid way, holding handkerchiefs.

"Why are you here?" I looked back at the others, who seemed to not realize I was away from them.

"No, they realize, they just cannot see you."

"Julian and Athena will worry."

"They will be okay. Now, the reason for my being here is a one-time favor for the voodoo queen herself. She asked me to bring you to see your friend one last time. I normally don't allow the living or anyone through to the seventh gate of Guinee without going through the others, but since you won't be staying, I see no harm." He smiled wickedly. "Now, don't you have something for me?"

"Oh yes." I handed him the bag.

He looked inside. "Perfect. Let's get going." He tipped his hat, smiled spookily, and walked in front of me, the tails on his tuxedo jacket flapping in the wind. "We don't have all day. If the others gatekeepers find out, I'm afraid dangerous spirits may be let loose to drag someone back with them, back to the land of the dead."

Chapter thirteen

Julian

In an instant, I went into full panic mode. The wind blew and whipped around me. My hair fell down around my shoulders. I removed my jacket and threw it, causing it to land on a nearby tomb. "Where the hell is Rosie?"

"Don't panic." A voice from behind me spoke. "She will be right back, she has some goodbyes to get out of the way." Marie smiled, her skirt blowing around her as did the leaves from the trees overhead.

"How?" Concern laced my voice.

"I asked a friend to help her say a true goodbye."

"She needs that."

"Yes, she does," she replied, never looking at me but in the direction of an old dilapidated mausoleum. Roots had taken hold of the fractured building, somehow stabilizing it. I ran over to it, but Marie stopped me and pulled me backward.

"She needs to do this on her own."

"But what if something happens to her?"

"Then she will have to figure out how to get herself out of the situation."

I turned to face the voodoo queen. "How can you be so blasé?" Anger threatened to show on my face.

"Young man, I am not being blasé; I am being realistic for your Rosie's benefit. Now I will forgive you for speaking to me like this one time, and one time only."

I hung my head in shame and worry for what she could do to me. I was already cursed due to my ancestor tricking her. This woman was not one to trifle with. I sighed, wishing I could run and get Rosie but knew better than to push it.

After the crowd had dispersed, I walked Jahane's mother and Derrick back to a car waiting to take them to the Brackish Tavern. "As soon as Rosie comes back we'll meet y'all at the Brackish Tavern."

"Thanks for everything." Mrs. Kellette hugged me and Derrick slid inside the car beside her.

The wait for Rosie to come back became pure torture. The shadows that danced across the tombs started to disappear as the red crispness of the sun descended behind the marble and trees. I walked back to the mausoleum and watched as Athena chased nonexistent things. I crossed my arms and kept an eye out for Rosie.

"They aren't nonexistent," Alma said beside me.

"What do you mean?"

"Open your eyes, boy, and you can see what she sees."

I focused my senses, all of them, on the dog, and slowly three or four apparitions came into view. I chuckled softly. "Well, I'll be." Athena chased and chased them. They flitted and floated above her, all the while staying away from her open mouth. The dog barked and barked. When she was done she plopped down on her belly on a small piece of grass and panted. Without even looking over at Alma I asked, "So those two do have a psychic connection?"

She laughed softly. "All witches who get a Guardian do."

I leaned up against the tomb and sighed. "That makes sense." All of a sudden Athena sat up and bounded off towards an old mausoleum.

Chapter fourteen

Rosie

I followed Baron Samedi through the old marble mausoleum. The stench of death caused me to choke and almost vomit. Off in the distance, a low chanting began.

Seven nights, seven moons, seven gates, seven tombs.

"Uh, who's chanting?" I asked the skeletal man.

He ignored me and kept walking. The rhyming followed us on our way. We went through tunnel after tunnel and a dozen passageways. My hands passed along the walls, and the strong smell of mold insulted my senses. Even though darkness shrouded us, somehow I saw my way. I chalked it up to the powerful loa in front of me. When I glanced down at the floor it seemed to be covered with something other than dirt. I cringed at the endless possibilities.

"Come, Rosaleigh." As I followed a cold breeze passed by me, but I also felt someone touch me.

"Ahh," I screamed.

The loa glanced over his shoulder and spoke to someone. "Leave her alone or you'll wish you had." Then it materialized in front of me, stuck its tongue out, and whizzed past me.

I continued my trek through the underground. A root popped out of the ground and I tumbled forward. As I slid my hand grasped the slick wall, but the skeleton man caught me before my face made contact with a half decomposed body. "Ugh." I shivered in disgust, and when I was firmly planted back on my feet I skirted around it. "What is this place?" I looked around in the pitch black with only a few flickering lights that reminded me of the fae, though I was sure that this was not the feu folette.

Baron Samedi turned around, his face slightly distorted. "This, my dear child, is the seventh gateway to the afterlife, or Guinee." He cackled and continued down the path.

The smell of rotting bodies followed us as we kept going. As I followed I dodged a few hundred spiders and slowly moved around one snake. It slithered past me, never paying attention. I blew a strand of hair from my face.

When I saw the proverbial light at the end of the tunnel, I sighed but continued. Baron Samedi stepped aside. "You have only a few minutes; use them wisely and quickly."

"Thank you." I walked around him and into the sunlight—or something similar to sunlight—and saw her as clear as day. I called out, "Jahane!"

She turned around and smiled. "Rosie, you are here?" She looked past me and nodded her head at the figure behind me. "Come sit, we don't have much time. I must get going."

I sat, and when I looked at her I saw that she wore the bracelet and the engagement ring. She twirled the ring on her finger around and around.

"I love the bracelet." She traced the diamond ring on her hand with a fingertip. "And tell Derrick I would've said yes."

I wiped a tear away. "How did you get them?"

She smiled up at me, that same smile I remembered from the first time we met. "The dead can do things the living can't comprehend. They just appeared on my wrist and finger."

"I'm so sorry."

"Don't be sorry, this is how it's supposed to be." She changed the subject. "Can you make sure Derrick is okay?"

"Anything for you."

She stopped fidgeting with the ring and looked up at me. "You will be fine, by the way. Your destiny has begun, and I see you overcoming so much. But your triumph will be hard, and only if you believe you can, you will win."

I saw murky water rising over her feet, but I ignored it and asked a question. "How do you know all this—?"

Before I finished a familiar voice spoke, "Jahane, it's time we go."

I turned around to see my mother, her long dark hair cascading over her shoulders. She stood in now ankle deep water.

"Mama."

She took me in her arms and held me tight. "Petal, remember you are strong. You don't need us anymore...you have Julian and Athena, who will be with you every step of the way." She pulled back and placed her hand over my chest. "Believe in your inner strength." She turned away from me, then back, wiping a tear that trickled down her face. "I love you. Find mine and your father's bodies. Don't let evil get the power that is yours."

"I promise, Mama."

I hugged Jahane for the last time ever. "I'll miss you."

"And I you."

Tears slid down my face as I watched them walk away and disappear. I sighed slightly, wringing my hands.

"Rosaleigh, we must go, the gate between the worlds is closing. We must go or deal with dangerous entities doing harm and dragging an unwilling body and soul to their death."

I stood and followed him out. After a long walk, I saw a smidge of light up ahead. When we stepped out of the mausoleum dusk peppered the sky with yellows, oranges, and reds. I turned and had a fleeting thought to hug him, but thought better of it. "Thank you for letting me say goodbye."

He dipped his head down, tipping his hat just a bit. His skeletal face smiled with a hint of mischief. The stench of rotting corpses escaped from his mouth and invaded my senses. "Be careful on the road ahead of you...it's full of twists and turns you may or may not be able to get out of."

All of a sudden Athena bumped into me.

"It's nice to see you again, Athena," the loa said, looking at my dog.

You too.

"Uh...how...?" I stopped. I wasn't even going to ask when she'd met the loa; it was better not knowing.

"Take care of your witch."

My Guardian bowed her head at the loa. *I'll do everything in my power.*

Chapter fifteen

Rosie

Julian ran to me when I exited the tomb. His face betrayed the elation he felt as he realized I was okay.

"Who's that?"

"Who?"

"That man walking off in the distance, the one wearing the black top hat." He turned around, and his skeletal face grinned maniacally at me. "Did you see that?"

"I did."

He quickly shook his head and changed the subject. "Where did you go?"

"To tell Jahane goodbye. Baron Samedi brought me," she said.

"Well, I'm just glad you are safe."

"Of course I am." I secretly hoped no evil had gotten past us.

"You ready to head on over to the Brackish Tavern?"

"Wait." I knelt down, resting my hand on the marble grave. From the corner of my eye, I saw a red lily. The petals fluttered, calling out to me. Julian stood behind me, his presence calming me as my body ached from the pain of losing my best friend. But this lone flower alive amongst so much death reminded me that there was something worth living for. I stood and pressed the fabric of my dress back into place."Yes." I leaned into him as we walked to the waiting car.

I slid in, and even though I probably seemed okay my heart felt heavy. But deep down I knew I would survive. The ride to the restaurant was quick, maybe because my thoughts about the last thing my mama said played over and over in my head.

We pulled up to the curb and Athena pushed the seat forward, jumping out of the car. *Hurry Mom, I'm starving.*

I laughed. "I'm sure Mr. Jacque has made something special just for you."

If not my friends will have my back.

"Your...fr...?"

Julian grabbed my hand. "Did you know that your dog plays with ghosts?"

"Yes." A lightbulb went off. "The Brackish Tavern has ghosts."

He laughed. "Cher—"

But I interrupted him. "Yes, I know...this is known as the city of the dead. Most everything in this city is haunted."

"Very true. Now let's get inside before Athena eats everything she can reach, which is...uh, yeah, everything." I chuckled as Julian held the door open for me.

The restaurant had been set up nicely with food on all the tables. "Rosie, oh Rosie." Mr. Jacque ran over to me and engulfed me in a hug. "I'm so sorry to hear about Jahane."

"Thank you, sir."

"Come in, come in, plenty of food, and I even set up a karaoke machine since the rumors are that was something she liked." He dropped his head, and when he picked it back up he dabbed at his eyes with a white handkerchief.

"You have always been so kind to us."

"Why not? You both are like my daughters. I'll miss her."

"Me too." I leaned in and whispered. "Sorry about Remi."

"Yes, he won't be easily replaced."

I winked at him. "Something tells me he'll be around." The corners of my mouth turned upwards as I saw Athena heading into the kitchen with a familiar figure.

"You may be right. You do know my restaurant is, some say, haunted." He quirked a brow at me. "Get some food, there's plenty." He walked away to make sure his guests had everything they needed.

My attention quickly diverted to the corner of the room, where Big Chief Mouton was huddled talking to Marie Laveau. "I'll be right back."

"Take your time, cher."

Before I made it to the pair, Miss Alina and Madam Claudette stopped me, both hugging me at the same time.

"Hello," my muffled voice said through their arms.

"Are you doing okay?" they said in unison.

I pushed back. "Yes." I turned my gaze back to the two people talking in the corner. "Do you know anything about him?" I nodded in the direction of the Mardi Gras Indian.

Madame Claudette grinned but never said a word.

"No need...I'll find out if something is off about him. He knows things and talks even more cryptically than you Madam Claudette."

Her eyebrows shot up. "What? Not possible. I'm queen of the cryptic."

I laughed loudly and the room went silent. Everyone turned to face me. "I'm sorry to carry on."

I walked over to Marie Laveau and the Mardi Gras Indian Chief. "Thanks for everything."

He tipped his head at me. "My pleasure, Rosie. I must bid you both farewell."

After he left, I turned to Marie and glowered. "If I didn't like you, I'd punish you for that look. But what's on your mind?"

"Tell me more about him." I nodded to the tall African man walking away.

"What would you like to know, mon piti?"

"For starters, how does he know about me?"

"Ah, that. He said you would ask more questions. Come sit." I sat, and even though it had gotten noisy I could hear her clearly. "It is said that Baron Samedi likes to flirt with human women. He is a dastardly fellow if I've ever met one. And unbeknownst to his wife, Maman Brigitte, he bedded a human woman."

"No!" I gasped.

"Yes, he did." She grinned, and for a second it was fearsome. "Anyway, he got her pregnant, and when the baby was born and Maman Brigitte found out, she demanded to see the baby. She had planned on killing the child, but to punish the woman she instead took him for half of the year. The other half he was allowed to see his mother. So he is half loa and half human. He has the powers of the loa and is a spy to make sure Baron does not stray again."

"Wow, so that's how he knows so much."

"Yes." She smiled. "Remember, though, that the loa are tricksters, especially Baron Samedi, and the chief, being his son, is one as well. Now, I think you, Julian, and Athena need to be getting home. There's a gathering of the coven at your place. I'll be around if I'm needed."

I stood. "Speaking of the loa of the dead, thank you for having him take me to see Jahane."

"It wasn't all me, but you are welcome. The chief was the one who asked me to ask if his father would allow you to see your friend one last time."

"Why do you think he did it?"

"No idea, mon piti." I shuddered at the possibility that perhaps I was tricked into going.

Athena bumped into me. *Hey, Mom, have you eaten yet?*

"No, and I'm famished." I followed her to a table. As I sat down a man in a suit with a blonde woman on his arm walked over to me.

"Are you Rosie Delacroix?"

"Yes, I am," I said, placing my fork down.

"I'm Jasper Lafavre, and this is my wife Daphne. I've heard so much about you. My condolences on the loss of your friends. If you ever need anything, please let us know." He handed me a card.

"I will, thank you."

He smiled and turned to leave.

From somewhere in the crowded room I heard my name. "Rosie." I looked up and saw the red head of my friend Andre. An old friend, Benjamin, followed him. Behind them was another dear friend, Midori. I stood up, planting a smile on my face as they made their way over to me.

"Oh, I can't believe about Jahane," Andre squealed and wrapped his arms around me.

"I know." I managed a grin. I held back tears but one slowly escaped.

Benjamin leaned down and hugged me. "Oh doll, don't cry," he said kindly. "I just got back to the city and we heard the horrific news."

I pulled back from his embrace. "Honestly, I didn't know I had many tears left. Yes, I'm still reeling over it."

He nodded. "Yes, but it will get better as the days fade."

He wiped away a tear. "Keep the memories alive, just don't live in them."

I changed the subject. "How are you, Benjamin? It's been too long."

"It has."

"So what have y'all been up to?" I asked.

Midori's face lit up but quickly fell. "We uh...."

I grabbed her hand. "It's okay, Midori. Jahane would have loved to know what y'all are up to."

She smiled and continued. "We are doing our own shows now. We have the TMI show hosted by Eureka and Liberaunchy. Plus a few other things. We're the drag queen and Beaux queen duo."

Tears bubbled at the news. "Jahane always loved a good drag show."

Benjamin leaned down. "Well, I'll tell you this, our next show we'll dedicate to her."

"She'd love that."

He smiled. "Good...no more tears. She'd want to know you are happy."

Athena nudged me. *Mom, who's this*?

I laughed. "Benjamin, Midori, I'd like to introduce you to Athena."

"Nice to meet you." Benjamin leaned down. "Hey, I think we've met before."

Athena sniffed him. The look on her face caused me to burst out laughing. *Mom, he smells familiar but looks different.*

Benjamin laughed. "I know where I've seen you. One day before a show. You were walking down the street."

I whispered to Athena. "You really need to stop going out by yourself. I think you met him when he was dressed as Eureka."

I don't understand.

"I'll explain later." I looked up at the two and smiled. "Thank you so much for stopping by. Have you had anything to eat? Athena and I will come by and see a show."

"We'll grab a bite, but we need to get back and ready for tonight. Please come check us out soon."

"I will."

"Before we go. Don't ever forget how lucky you are."

"How?"

"You had a best friend who truly cared about you. That's hard to come by nowadays." He nodded to Midori. "Isn't that right?"

She came over and hugged me. Her lips curved upwards. "It sure is. I treasure Benjamin every day."

"Hey, what about me? Am I chopped liver?" Andre spoke up.

The two chuckled and Benjamin grabbed him by the shoulders and tugged him closer. "You know we adore you. Hell, if not for you I'd never have found Blaine."

"True. I'll always be a bridesmaid never a bride." Andre grinned.

"Pfft, you'll find someone."

I nodded as they left, then turned to Athena. *You ready to go home?* she asked.

"I am, are you? Have you had enough to eat?"

Yes, Mom. She licked a few remnants of cheese off her muzzle. I assumed she had eaten a whole plate of cheese fries, courtesy of my best friend.

"Night, Madame Laveau."

"Night, Rosie and Athena."

As I walked through the room I saw Derrick, so I walked over to him. "By the way, she would've said yes."

His eyes brightened and tears filled them. "Thank you for that."

"I miss her too." As the words came out I hugged him tight, then Julian came up behind us.

"Be safe, Rosie."

"I will."

Chapter sixteen

Julian

We remained silent on the drive home, but when we pulled up to the curb it sounded like a party was going on in the courtyard. Rosie and Athena both jumped out of the car and ran. "Wait, you two."

"We can't," Rosie yelled over her shoulder.

I locked the car and ran to catch up. When I did, the sight before me was like nothing I'd seen before...and lately, I'd seen a lot of crazy shit. The courtyard was lined with chairs in a crescent shape. At least a dozen or so tiny lights bounced up and down above us. On further inspection, I saw people in the balls of light. They held swords or knives and were dressed in military garb.

"What is all this?"

"Hello, you must be Julian," a woman in black addressed me. "Alma has told us so much about you."

"Nice to meet you..uhm...?"

"Where are my manners? I am Elspeth and this is Marron. We are from Rosie's coven." She pointed to the woman standing beside her.

"Nice to meet you both. Can you tell me what's going on here?" I scanned the courtyard and noticed a few more people that I didn't recognize.

"In time, dear boy. Come, sit with us." They stood on either side of me and looped their arms into mine. "Some of these witches here are from your coven; they have come out of hiding." I glanced over at Rosie, who was talking to Alma. "Don't worry, she will be fine."

I sat and Alma walked in front of the fountain that I now saw spurting blue and green illuminated water. Rosie stood beside her. "I bring this meeting of the Bayou and Crescent Coven's together. As we all know, Rosie's mother and leader of the Crescent Coven passed to the other side today." She nodded in my direction. Elspeth and Marron nudged me forward. "Julian, come here."

I stood and hesitantly walked over to them. Rosie linked her fingers with mine. "As those of you from the Bayou Coven have heard the rumors, Julian Quibadeaux has regained his powers as a witch after nullifying the curse he was born with." Rosie squeezed my hand in reassurance.

One by one the witches from my coven came up to me, each offering me an item. As they stood in front of me I looked up into the sky and saw that it was filled with the illumination from millions of stars. Alma and Rosie stepped out of the way as the members encircled me and began a spell.

In this circle we call home.
Where only those invited roam.
We raise our power together as one.
This induction has begun.
For some time we've watched him grow.
Into great strength and power, we know.
We welcome in with arms open wide.
We as a coven are here to guide.
Look deep inside here and now.
Accept our offer and make your vow.

One of my coven members stepped forward. "Now Julian, in our coven you must vow with blood. As you do please repeat after me."

He handed me a silver handled knife. I turned to Rosie and she nodded. With the blade in my hand, I sliced through my palm.

With these words here and now.
I accept entrance with a vow.
To the coven I will be true.
And have pride and honor in all I do.
Never alone. Together we stand.
I seal my vow with a drop of blood from my hand.

Once I was done they nodded in unison. "We are done." They returned to their seats and Rosie walked back over to me and grasped my hand.

"You two can take a seat with the others." We walked to the only two empty seats in the middle. "Okay, witches and fairies." Alma looked up at the balls of lights dancing back and forth. "It has come to my attention that we have a unique evil brewing in the city. I fear something we thought we had rid the world of has been lurking in plain sight of us all."

I whispered to Rosie. "What is she talking about?"

"I've no idea."

Alma continued. "I fear the witch we all know as Yvette is in actuality a succubus."

Gasps and oh no's filled the courtyard. "It can't be," Elspeth retorted.

"Everyone calm down and sit back down." Alma waved her hands down. Then she turned her head and nodded. A figure walked out, and at first sight of my brother I lunged forward from my chair.

"What the hell are you doing here?"

"Give him a chance to speak."

I saw that his hands were bound as he walked into the middle. I stood back but remained on high alert. "Fine."

Dax began to speak. "As you all know, my mother is Yvette my father is Marcel Quibadeaux."

"Hurry up with this shit so I can rip you to pieces," I interrupted him.

"Be careful, brother, or you may turn no matter what's on your finger." He turned back to the crowd. "Anyway, as I was saying before I was so rudely interrupted." He smirked to the crowd. "I've come across some interesting papers and books in my grandfather Henri's study. One that speaks of a woman who can bend any man to her will. The picture resembled my mother. When I went to confront her, I found a tomb that I'd not known of before."

"Why are you helping us?" I interrupted him.

"Because as much as I want it, I will never be Henri's second in command, so I want to destroy him and my mother."

I nodded, not sure I believed him. No way in hell was I going to trust this asshole.

"Wait…if what you say is true, what do we do about her, Alma? I mean, we thought we'd already rid the world of succubi," Elspeth asked.

"With Rosie and Julian." She looked over at us. "You've already come in contact with her and were able to push off her advances."

"What do you mean?" Then the memories flooded through me. The woman by the tree that night in the bayou. I had pushed her off, but it had taken a second. And Gabby with her incessant flirting when they kidnapped me. I looked over at Alma and sighed. "How come I was able to reject her?"

"Because, Julian, you are dual natured." I cocked my head, not fully understanding. She laughed. "You are a witch and a rougaroux, as is your brother, though in his case he's a succubus and a rougaroux."

I interrupted. "Speaking of dear brother...." I peered over at him. "How come you haven't changed?"

"How do you know I haven't?" he sneered. "If I had managed to kill you like Henri wanted I would be different right now. But like you, I'm dual natured."

"That's enough, you two," Alma chastised.

My attention suddenly diverted to Rosie. Out of the corner of my eye, I saw her watching Athena. Then she ran towards the dog.

Chapter seveneen

Rosie

As Julian and Dax argued I look frantically around for Athena. The tiny hairs on the back of my neck rose. Something was wrong. I called out to my Guardian. "Athena."

But her attention was focused on something else. She padded over to a bright orange and red marigold I hadn't noticed before. Athena cocked her head and sniffed the flower. A buzzing noise reverberated off the brick walls of the courtyard.

"No Athena!" I screamed and ran over to her as she dropped to the ground. All the witches formed a barrier around us. Black smoke swirled and puffed into the circle, and held her off the ground. As I looked into the smoke I saw a hideous face staring back at me with a maniacal toothless grin. The smell of sulfur and decay permeated around us.

"Put her down!"

The figure cloaked in smoke turned to me. "Witch, you will not speak to me in that tone or tell me what I will or will not do."

I didn't back down. "I'll speak however I like, and you will let down my Guardian." I enunciated each word emphatically. The wind began to howl around me and the walls shook. Some bricks loosened from the wall and ground as my anger increased.

The figure dangled Athena in the air. "No, I will take my body and soul for your disturbance in Guinee."

"Then you go find another one." My anger heightened and the spirit flew backward, hitting the fountain and causing water and stone to explode all over.

He or she stood in a fighting stance. "Little witch, you do not know who you are messing with."

"Find someone else, the dog is not going with you." I was not going to back down no matter what. I'd had enough people taken from me lately.

The creature stood back, then laughed eerily and let Athena go. Before she crashed to the cobblestone, I let my powers safely place her down. "Fine." He pointed a bony finger in my face, his putrid breath making my eyes water and my stomach want to hurl. "But I'll give you till the next full moon to find me a replacement." A loud crack and boom resonated off the walls and the spirit was gone.

As it disappeared, I choked on the stench of decay. Turning around I saw the grim expressions and chuckled nervously. "We won't fret about this. First, we'll find out what happened to Athena and make her better. Second, we will find my parents' bodies. Last, we will worry about the angry spirit demanding a body to drag down to the underworld."

A young witch from Julian's coven stepped forward. "I know of a vet from Puerto Rico I can call."

"What's your name?" I asked.

"Apris," she replied meekly.

"Nice to meet you."

"I'll give her a call." The young witch dug into her pocket and pulled out her phone.

Miss Alina knelt down. "I fear this is the work of Gabby, maybe on the word of her mother."

"I agree."

Julian spoke up. "Let's get Athena somewhere comfortable." I passed a hand over her fur; she didn't move, but her chest continued to move up and down in synchronized rhythm. Julian hoisted her up into his arms and carried her up the steps. I followed and tried to hide my worry.

Once in my room, he placed her on the bed. "She'll be safe in here."

"Yes, I think so." I crawled into the bed and lay beside her. Nuzzling my face into her soft coat, I whispered, "This can't be happening." Exhaustion resided in my body and I closed my eyes. I snuggled next to her, placing my arm over her body. Before I fell asleep, Julian pulled the blanket over us.

Chapter eighteen

Julian

A slight knock echoed on the door. I patted Rosie and kissed her on the cheek, then answered the door. When I opened it, Apris stood there.

"Julian, I spoke with the vet who specializes in magical creatures. She is trying to catch a flight now."

"When can we expect her?"

"Hopefully sometime tomorrow."

"Good. Now, want to help me figure out what kind of poison put Athena in this situation?"

She cocked her head at me. "How do you know she was poisoned?"

I scoffed. "Because as we all know, Athena is extremely powerful, so this is the only explanation." I stepped outside, shutting the door behind me.

We walked outside, where darkness shrouded the courtyard except for two fairies keeping watch over our home. I glanced over to them, nodding my approval. One flew down, landing on the ground.

"King Roi asked us to stay and keep an eye out."

"Tell him his kindness and protection are appreciated."

I walked over to the yellow and orange flower that seemed to have caused all the doom tonight. On closer inspection, the harmless looking flower had some white residue covering the petals.

"Don't touch it!" Miss Alina said as she came out from the store. As she ran over to us, she let the screen door slam against the frame.

I backed away. "I didn't know you were still here."

"Yes, I was in the shop using the phone so as not to disturb Rosie. I've been in the shop trying to get in touch with Alexander."

I looked at her. "Who?"

"The alchemist who created Athena. Maybe he can help us figure this out. After all, he created her."

"Apris called a vet who specializes in magical creatures."

"The more the better." She nodded her head.

"We have to heal Rosie's Guardian." I sighed, knowing that if we lost Athena, Rosie would never recover. Too much death and loss.

Miss Alina walked over to me and placed her hand on my forearm. "We will. Then we will find Magnolia and Rosie's father's bodies."

"Speaking of, where is my brother?"

"Locked up in a secret place."

"Y'all don't trust him either?"

"No, we don't...he is the son of a succubus, after all. I know Alma wants to believe he has some good qualities, but I swore to Magnolia that I would protect her daughter."

"As did I." I exhaled. "So did you get in touch with Alexander?"

"Yes, I did. He should be here sometime after the vet gets here. Maybe together they can heal Athena."

"Good." I hugged her.

"Julian, you should get some rest. Rosie and Athena will need you at your best," she said as she looked at the deadly flower and pulled it magically from the dirt. It floated over to an open plastic Baggie. She faced Apris. "Come on, hun, we have hotel rooms for all the visiting witches. We must all get some rest and keep our strength up for Rosie and Athena."

"Goodnight." I turned around and headed back up the stairs and into the house to check on Rosie and her beloved Guardian.

Chapter nineteen

Rosie

later that night I woke to find my Guardian still in a coma. I rolled over and saw the moonlight shining through a crack in the drapes. Why would anyone do this? Then in an instant, I knew I was being distracted from finding my parents' bodies. I sat up, leaned in, and kissed her on the head. Her soft fur tickled my nose. Nuzzling my face further into her coat, I let a tear fall. It settled and finally disappeared deep into her hair.

I pulled back and slowly inched off the bed, not wanting to disturb Athena. As I stood, I willed myself not to cry...I had to be strong. I strode over to the door leading outside and slipped out.

Fairies floated above me in formation, guarding the perimeter. Two of them stood by the iron gates leading to the courtyard. One flew down to me, placed his arrow into his quiver, and bowed to me. "Captain Eloi at your service. I am in charge of the sentries. May I help you with something?"

I glanced over at him. "No thank you. Why are y'all still here?" He looked abashed. "Not that I mind." I quickly grinned.

He returned the smile. "We have strict orders from King Roi to stay here and protect you and your family."

"I would like to one day thank your king. He's come to my rescue more than once now."

The fairy sentry bowed his head. "I shall inform him of your request."

I yawned. "I would appreciate that."

"You should get back inside. We will be watching over your home, and will warn you of any impending attacks."

I nodded and crept back inside. Julian sat on the bed petting, Athena. He turned and sadness enveloped his face.

"How is she?" I inquired.

"Same, nothing has changed."

I sat down on the bed and he took my hand. "I hope we can save her." I started to worry again.

"We will wake her, I promise," he said, squeezing my hand. His finger touched my chin and he lifted my head up. "A vet who specializes in magical creatures is on her way. Also,

Alexander, who created Athena, is headed here as well."

"Wait—?" Before I could speak he pulled me closer to him.

"Miss Alina called him. Why don't we get some rest? We have a big day ahead of us."

"Sure, but I don't know if I can sleep."

"Try...for me."

I nodded and scooted down between him and Athena. My head rested against his arm and I fell asleep.

Voices pulled me from my sleep so I rolled over. The light blinded me from the open drapes. How long had I been asleep? I stretched, arching my back, trying to remove the ache deep inside. Athena lay on the bed, still out, but her chest continued to move up and down. I kissed her head then scooted out of the bed.

Once I walked out, I could make out more of the conversation taking place in my living room. Sitting around were three people I didn't recognize. The man had red hair and a nicely trimmed beard to match. The woman who sat beside him petted one fawn puppy that sat on her lap. Another one sprawled himself across the rest of the couch. A giant blue Great Dane sat beside the man. Over to the left sat a woman with dark hair and wide eyes.

"Rosie, good you are awake." Miss Alina came over to me. "I'd like to introduce you to Dr. Riella Roman."

The woman stood and offered her hand to me. "Nice to meet you," she said in a thick Spanish accent.

I nodded, still not totally awake. "Same here. Do you think you can save my dog?"

"Yes, with—" She was interrupted as she looked over at the woman standing beside me.

Miss Alina's expression grew excited as Alexander stood from the sofa. He confidently walked over towards us, the Great Dane following him. "This is Alexander. He created Athena and Ares." She waved to the blue dog.

Alexander extended his hand to me. "Rosie, I am truly sorry we are meeting under these circumstances."

Tears formed in my eyes. "Nice to meet you too. I'm sorry I let this happen to her."

He held onto my hand. "Oh dear, this is not your fault," he said in a thick German accent.

The other woman walked over to me, one puppy in her arms as the other one jumped off the sofa, sliding on the hardwood floor. He caught sight of Ares' tail and started to bat at it as he swished it back and forth.

I saw the woman exchange looks with Miss Alina. "Rosie, I'm Alisa. We will find out what has caused her to be asleep and fix this."

I looked down, and the dog called Ares was gone. I glanced at the door to my room as a grey-blue tail disappeared behind the closing door. She laughed. "Don't worry, he's just going to say hello to his sister."

I wiped my eyes as Julian held on to me. After a quick breakfast cooked by Alma, we all headed out to the shop, minus Alisa and the dogs.

"You aren't coming?" I asked.

"No dear, I'll keep an eye on Athena and the other Guardians. It's my job as keeper of the Guardians."

"Are you sure...?"

She chuckled as she patted the dog in her arms. The puppy blinked its eyes then yawned, only to nestle back further into her arms. "Don't worry...I have gypsy magic to hold off anything that threatens to attack." She leaned in and hugged me, careful not to squish the puppy.

"Thanks, Alisa."

We headed outside through the courtyard to the shop. I figured in all of the old stuff Mama had kept, she maybe had some items Alexander could use.

The courtyard looked somewhat different this morning, but I couldn't quite put my finger on it. Perhaps it had to do with the broken fountain or the dozen or so floating fairies above us. A few of them, though, were stationed on the ground with bows and arrows. I glanced up and saw Eloi, and he saluted me and went to check on the boundaries.

I shook my head and headed towards the shop. I unlocked the door and we filed inside. Alexander walked in behind me, as did Miss Alina. He turned to her.

"Do you have the flower that Athena sniffed?" Alexander asked.

"Yes, I'll go get it." Miss Alina ran into the store room to get it.

He turned to Julian. "Grab my bag over there."

He pointed to a huge black bag by the wall. Julian picked up the bag and placed it on the table, then opened it and peered inside. Alexander came over and began taking items out—a candle, an old fashioned bunsen burner, as well as three or four glass bottles—and placed them on the table. While Julian helped him I ran over to the windows and closed the blinds so we wouldn't be disturbed.

Miss Alina came out with a baggie containing the marigold. She held it with her thumb and forefinger as if the flower inside would poison her through the bag. Carefully she put it on the table.

Alexander slid gloves over his hands and emptied the flower onto a clear square plate that floated above the table. It reminded me of a big coaster. The flat object had no sides and had a magical appearance, but soon sides began to form, encasing the flower that floated, unmoving, above the bottom. It began to bounce off the sides as if it wanted out of its prison.

Alexander turned and saw the expression on my face. "It's to make sure we don't contaminate the flower."

I stood back and watched as he performed test after test, warming the glass bottles and swooshing the liquid around in them. After each test, he reported his findings to Dr. Riella, who was busily writing it all down in a notebook.

"Doctor, I can't seem to distinguish between two important factors."

"Alexander, we'll get it."

I sat back and sipped a cup of hot tea and read from one of the books on the shelves as the two worked busily together.

"Dammit!" Alexander stood, causing his chair to tumble backward onto the floor.

"What's wrong?"

I closed the book and sat up, turned around, and saw a small fire burning on the table. He quickly scooped what was left of the flower out of the way. Dr. Riella sprinkled something on the flames and they died.

Alexander sat back down, never answering me. He just buried his head in his hands. My heart stuck in my chest at the possibility of not finding a cure for my Guardian. After a few minutes, he looked up. "Wait, Riella...I think we were off by a small calculation on a cure."

"How much off?"

He showed her something and I careened my head to see, but could not make any sense of his scribblings.

"Ah, we fix this here, and this, and we have it." She wrote on the piece of paper.

"Yes, you are right." He jotted something down on a paper. "Julian, can you call on one of your coven members to pick up the items on this list?"

"Yes, I'll call Apris. See if she knows where to get these." He took the paper and kissed me on the mouth. "I'll be right back. I'll accompany her to get these."

I looked over to Alexander. "Do you think it will work?"

His expression was unreadable. "Rosie, I do believe we can cure Athena."

Chapter twenty

Julian

I knocked on the hotel room door and Apris greeted me. "Yes, Julian, how can I help you?"

"I need to know if you know how to get these items." I handed her the slip of paper and she scanned it, then nodded.

"So Dr. Riella has arrived?"

"Yes, early this afternoon, along with Alexander. Do you have any idea where to get this stuff?"

"Yes, I do."

"Where?"

She laughed. "I'm surprised that you've never heard."

"How would I?"

"True. You've just found out you are a witch. There are rumors that your mother kept an old camp out in the Manchac Swamp with healing plants and herbs. I have never seen the place, but my ancestors swear it exists. I only know where it's supposed to be located, and have no idea if it's been kept up. Like I said, it was a rumor."

"But a rumor worth checking out."

"Yes, let me get my purse." She left the door cracked but soon returned. "Ready?"

I nodded. "The faster we do this, the sooner Rosie can relax."

Once we were in the car, I turned to her. "So where are we going?"

"Manchac Swamp, of course." She laughed at me as if I was not catching on to this whole magical world.

The ignition roared to life as I turned the key, and I pulled the car out and headed towards the interstate. I didn't speak much on the trip, only because my mind was elsewhere.

"Here, turn right." I did as she instructed, and we pulled down a gravel road. "Take a left." My hands on the steering wheel, I manoeuvred down the road. "We're here." I saw nothing except for an old skiff that looked as if it had seen better days, the paint chipped in blotches all over. "Come on, hurry," she said impatiently.

We jumped out of the car and headed over to the boat. "Let me get it started." I pulled the rope six or seven times before the boat puttered to life. I backed up and headed through the swamp. "Where are we going?" She didn't answer me, just kept her gaze ahead of us, in some sort of trance. After about fifteen minutes, I asked a different question. "How much longer?"

"Not much...wait...." She looked up in the sky and it opened up. "What the hell is going on?"

The rain pelted down around us, causing the water to splash up into the boat. "I think someone is trying to stop us," I yelled over the thundering rain.

"You think?" She grimaced.

Thunder boomed and lightning cracked above us. A bolt of lightning missed the boat by mere feet, but it lit up the murky water around us. I glanced down and saw gators swimming around underneath, waiting for the right time to catch their prey. The sudden storm pushed the boat around in the water, and as it threatened to tip over, the alligators chomped at us. As the boat pushed through the waters, I flew backward and hit the outboard motor connected to the stern. Once I regained my balance I looked down and saw blood seeping from a gash on my elbow. I tried to take control of the boat before it capsized and sent us into the gator infested waters.

As we maneuvered through the bayou, the branches of the trees reached out for us, threatening to wrap themselves around our necks to choke us. The Spanish moss blew off the trees, covering us in its gray tendrils. I heard it before I saw it...the hiss of a huge water moccasin. Its mouth opened wide and it lunged at me. Before it bit down I grabbed it and squeezed tight. It fought back but could not stop me from pulling it apart. Blood spattered me and I wiped it from my face. The scent of copper permeated the air around me.

The boat continued to rock back and forth, dipping further into the water. Apris held onto the side of the boat, trying her best not to fall in. One gator jumped up and took a bite out of the boat, catching Apris in the arm.

"Julian!" she screamed as it dragged her off into the water.

"Apris!" I screamed. I jumped into the water and swam after her. The gator quickly dragged her underneath, spinning around and around as he went further underwater, trying to drown his prey. Water splashed around us as Apris tried to fight. Another gator swam towards me. Quickly anger consumed me, and the gator slid backward in the water.

The torrential rainstorm pounded down on me as I dove back down into the water and came eye to eye with the alligator. Apris' body hung limply from his jaws. Before I could stop myself I thought about death to this animal. As quickly as that the alligator let go of Apris and exploded. Not hesitating or thinking about the blood and guts floating on top of the water, I grabbed Apris and pulled her to the surface.

When I had her safely back above the murky deep water, the bobbing pieces of alligator hide surrounded us. The scent of blood and rotting fish coated my nostrils as I glanced around for any more reptiles wanting to eat us. Realizing if we stayed there any longer they could come back to attack, I looked around for the boat. "Shit, shit." The storm must have pushed it away.

I kept Apris' head above the water as much as possible and swam to the nearest levy. I became tired and my body slowed. Finally, I dragged her body up the embankment. She lay flat and I quickly checked her pulse. "Shit," I muttered to myself. I began the proper procedure to rid her lungs of the water. After what felt like an eternity, she choked and spit up water. I brushed her wet hair back from her face. "Are you okay?"

She coughed some more and tried to sit up. "I think so."

"Apris...no you aren't, you're bleeding."

She glanced down at her arm. "Oh, that's nothing." She grimaced, her face squinching up in pain.

"That's not nothing, Apris. That gator almost killed you."

"But it didn't. Now we need to get to your mother's place."

"That can wait...we need to get you to a doctor. Anyway, I think either Yvette or Gabby tried to stop us, and they probably know about my mother's secret stash."

I looked over to my right through the trees that hid us and saw a figure standing on a small bridge, their hands high in the air. I couldn't make out who it was, but there was no doubt in my mind that it was either Yvette or Gabby.

"How do you know?"

I pointed. "See there."

"Oh, hell no." She waved her hands, but I stopped her.

"No Apris, we can't beat her. We need Rosie."

"Julian, you have powers too."

"Yes, but...," I screamed over the torrential rain that had started again. "I don't know exactly what those are."

She looked over at me and back at the figure. Then she looked over at the bloody water and pieces of gator littering the murky water. The stench of eviscerated gator permeated the swamp waters. "I think I know one of your powers," she smirked, her eyes closing to slits.

The rain came down harder and I screamed, "We are more powerful with help."

My soaked hair hung dripping on my shoulders and on my face. I pushed it back and rung it out.

"Okay." She surrendered and tried to stand up but wobbled.

"Wait, you've lost a lot of blood. We need to stop the bleeding." I noticed the huge gash in her arm, and though I didn't have time to inspect it much, I knew I needed to get her help. I ripped the bottom of my shirt off, squeezed the water out, and wrapped it tightly around her arm, hoping to stop the bleeding. "Okay, that should work until we get back. Now to find our way back to the car."

She managed a weak smile, her face turning pale. "I can help with that." With a slight wave of her hand, a small light bounced along in front of us. "Come on, Julian, let's go." She tried to stand but I stopped her.

"Wait. You need to conserve your energy to get us back to the car." I scooped her up. "This will be faster; just keep that going." I inclined my head to the light ahead. She leaned against me and her eyes shut every few steps I took, but the ball of light kept going. We followed the bouncing light dashing around the trees. After about an hour the car appeared where we had left it. I slid her into the car. "Now let's get you back and bandaged up."

Chapter Twenty-one

Julian

I waited outside patiently for Julian to arrive back home. His car pulled up to the curb and he exited, carrying Apris. One of her arms had been bandaged, but blood seeped through what looked like part of Julian's shirt.

"What happened? Did you get everything?" I babbled.

"No cher." He rushed past me. "Where is everyone? We need to get her some help."

One of the sentries came running up. "Hi, I'm Amos, I'll take her inside and look after her." He took Apris from him, and I grabbed Julien's arm. He wrapped his strong muscled arms around me.

"What if we can't help her?" He held me as I felt an inexplicable pain course through me. My heart broke.

"Don't worry, cher, we will."

"What happened?"

"As we got closer someone tried to stop us. I fear it was either Gabby or Yvette." He tipped my head back. "Don't worry, cher, I'll do everything in my power to save Athena."

"But...." I stepped back and dropped to my knees, my body convulsing with yet another fear of heartache.

Julian knelt down and pulled me back up. "We just have to have another plan."

The sentry started to walk away. "Wait," Apris said. "Rosie, I agree with him, we need to formulate another plan. Besides, I think we have uncovered one of his powers."

I faced her. "What do you mean?"

"As a gator tried to pull me under, Julian saved me."

I turned to him. "How?"

"I don't know. I just thought of the alligator dead and it ended up in a dozen or so pieces."

"Wow."

She continued. "Yes. Your powers, Rosie, are rooted in the five elements. His are seated in the psyche. It seems as if he has the power of telekinesis."

"That's impressive."

"Yes it is," he retorted. "Now we need to get you inside and healed."

121

"I agree, Apris. Take her inside," I instructed the sentry. I grabbed Julian's hand and we entered the back of the shop.

Alexander and Dr. Riella sat by the table but stood when we entered. "Did you have any luck in acquiring—?" But he stopped as the sentry carried Apris inside. "What happened?"

"An alligator."

Amos placed her down on the sofa. "Don't worry, I can heal her." He pulled off the bandage. The blood had stopped, but her arm looked bad.

"Will she be okay?" I asked.

He smiled. "We fae have healing powers."

"Wait...." My thoughts went back to my Guardian. "Couldn't you heal Athena?"

The sentry stood. "Miss Rosie, we do have powers. I have been enlisted to help, but it will take more than what I offer to help your Guardian. Her's is a multitude of different reasons, magic, and poisoning." He turned back to Apris and pulled out some sparkly dust from a small pouch.

Alexander pulled us away from the sentry and witch. "So what happened?"

Julian hung his head. "I think either Gabby or Yvette tried to stop us. They started a storm and called perhaps every alligator in the vicinity to attack us. They knew we were there, probably even what we searched for."

"Well dammit." Our heads whipped around, and I saw Alisa standing by the door. "She's at it again. Gabby."

"How do you know it was her?"

"I had a vision of her."

"I hate that bitch," I spat.

"So do I. She has been a thorn in my side. And she is determined to get rid of Athena."

"Well, I will not allow it. She has to be stopped."

Alisa walked over to me. "We will stop her, I vow it."

"Speaking of Athena, how is she?"

"She is resting comfortably but is still unconscious. Ares is with her now. He is reminiscing with her about their time together so long ago."

I turned to Julian. "Y'all come up with a plan; I'm going to check on Athena."

"Sure, cher." He kissed me.

Upstairs I walked into the room but didn't see Athena. "Oh my goodness, where the hell is she?" I also didn't see Ares. I thought he was supposed to be watching her. In seconds a wave of panic rammed into me. I barely made it to the bed as my legs became like jelly.

"What's wrong?"

"Who's there?" I looked around and didn't see anyone. But when I focused I saw a white-haired man sitting beside the bed.

"Who are you and where is my Guardian?"

"In the bed."

I looked. "No, she's not.

He chuckled. "Rosie—"

But I didn't let him finish. "Who are you?" I asked again. The walls began to shake.

His kind smile lightened up his face. "I'm Karl, an old friend of Athena's and Alexander's."

"Why are you here?"

"To watch over her."

I sat on the bed and reached out, but felt nothing for a second. Then as I moved my hand around it touched something soft. Slowly Athena came into view. She lay on her side, her eyes closed. I laughed, remembering that she could make herself invisible. "Why is she doing this?" I asked as she disappeared again.

"I assume as a defense mechanism in case she's in danger while she's out."

She came back again and I petted her. "Smart dog."

"Yes, that she is."

"Where is Ares?"

"He stepped out to let me have a little time with her...he'll be back." Karl dropped his head and looked wistful. "You know, I knew she was destined for greatness." He petted her head as she came into view again. "That is why they are after her and you. With her, you can stand against evil."

Julian interrupted us. "Cher, we have a plan. Come, we must prepare."

I faced Karl and he petted Athena. "She'll be fine...I'll watch over her."

"Are you sure?"

He nodded. "Yes, I promise."

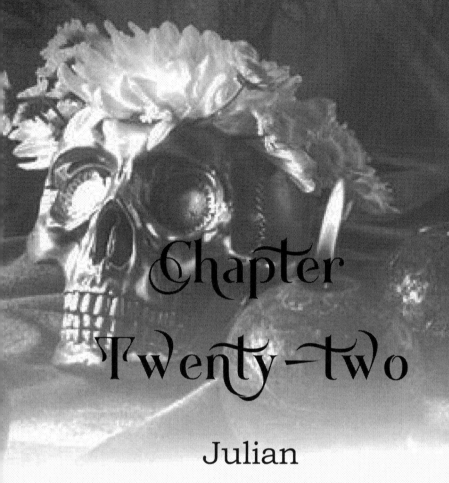

Chapter Twenty-two

Julian

I watched as Rosie headed to check on her Guardian, then turned to Alexander. "What happened?" he asked.

"When we got there we were immediately stopped."

"No doubt Gabby and her mother will do whatever it takes to stop Rosie," Alisa interjected.

"I'm afraid so. Since they know what we are after, I'm afraid they may have gotten rid of whatever we need."

"I doubt that," Apris spoke up.

I had my hands crossed over my chest. "What do you mean?"

"Julian, do you remember I told you it was a rumor? Who do you think started the rumor?"

"My mother?"

She nodded. "Yes. So don't you think she would have a backup?"

"Let's hope you are right, for Athena's sake. So do we have a plan?"

"I think I have something. I can place a cloaking spell around us so that they can't detect us or the boat. Then you and Rosie will go get what we need," Apris said confidently.

"That's it?"

She laughed. "Yes, we won't be seen. Now go get Rosie."

As Rosie and I headed outside into the courtyard, we were met with a few fairy sentries. One flew down and stepped out of his ball of light. "Master Julian and Mistress Rosie, I send my second in command Amos to go with you on your trek."

"Thank you."

"I will stay here and guard the dog."

Rosie hugged the sentry. "Thanks, Captain Eloi."

Alexander walked out with Dr. Riella and a few dozen potion bottles. "Here...in case you meet up with either Gabby or Yvette, you can use these. One is to drop them in their tracks. We fear they will divide and conquer. The majority of us will stay here and protect Athena. We'll send you, Rosie, and Apris with three sentries."

The bluish gray dog trotted outside and went up to Alexander. The majestic creature looked as if he didn't take any crap. He leaned into the man. At that moment I deduced Alexander also had a telepathic connection with Ares. He chuckled. "It seems as if Ares would like to go with you. He will help you as Athena helped Rosie."

We started to leave but Alexander stopped me and placed his hands on my shoulders. "Julian, use your powers," he said stoically.

"But—"

He waved his hands and stopped me. "Trust in yourself."

Julian, believe him. The gruff voice of Ares echoed in my head.

I stopped and looked over at Rosie. "Did you hear that?" I asked her.

She shook her head. "No, but we must go."

The dog walked in front of me. *She can't hear me unless I talk to her. Now I'm talking to you.*

"Why?"

Because you need my help.

I slapped my forehead and followed the dog and the others to the car.

We all squeezed into my car and drove back out to where the skiff had been. A big johnboat sat on the edge of the water. This time we would bring an element of surprise.

When we got out of the car Rosie leaned in. "You've got to believe in yourself."

"I know, cher." I kissed her. When our lips touched electrical currents passed through my body to hers. She pulled me closer to her, our souls latched onto each other. They fed off of each other. We were joined in more than one way. Our magic had intertwined together.

When she pulled back she looked up at me and smiled. "Why are you kissing me like it will be the last time?"

I chuckled. "Don't I always kiss you like that?"

"Yes, but that one had a little more...umm...something to it."

"Maybe it's just my powers surfacing."

"Maybe so. Now let's go kick some bitch ass." She stepped into the boat.

I helped Apris into the boat and waited for Ares to board, then I followed. Before I pulled the rope to start the motor I turned to Apris. "You ready?"

She nodded, then spoke a few words.

Words quickly spoken for a spell to rise.
So those chosen have unseeing eyes.
Make invisible this vessel and all those within.
To keep them safe make them now hidden.

As soon as the cloak was up I pulled the rope, and after three tries the boat purred to life. We quietly made our way out into the swamp. The three sentries flew ahead, keeping a keen eye out.

The calm water lapped up at the sides of the boat. The further we maneuvered the more my anticipation surfaced. A few dozen thoughts popped into my head. Finally, a rickety old house on stilts came into view sitting within the marsh.

"There it is," Apris whispered.

I pulled the boat up and docked it quietly. "Ares, you be on the lookout. Apris, keep the cloak up." She nodded. "Can you do it even if we are out of the boat?"

"Yes. It will take plenty of concentration, but I can do it."

I glanced up at the sentries. "You know what to do."

They saluted us and floated above the boat, and stayed high up to keep a lookout for things that could arise.

Rosie and I stealthily got out. We were quiet as we climbed the ladder to the wooden planked deck. My hand wrapped around the knob and it turned with a click. We entered and Rosie gasped at the site we stumbled into. We walked through the disheveled house, stepping over broken shards of glass and splintered wood on the floor. She screamed as she stepped into a hole in the floor. In two strides I made it over to her.

"Are you okay?"

"I think so," she whispered.

I pulled her up and checked her out, then handed her a potion and kept one clenched in my hand. "Do you see anything?"

"No, not yet."

I followed her around and out back, where we hit the motherload. The back porch was covered with buckets and containers of different types of flowers and herbs.

"I think this is it." I tore off half the paper with the ingredients. "Here, you look for half and I'll get this half."

Quickly we got busy finding everything. After we stuffed everything in a brown paper bag we snuck out. Rosie stopped suddenly.

"What is it?"

"Look!"

I watched where Rosie pointed. A figure dressed in black, her blonde hair blowing in the wind, was only mere feet from us.

"Is that...?" I whispered.

"Yes, Yvette. Well shit, that means Gabby is trying to get Athena." Her voice filled with panic.

"Then we must get back now. Be careful, cher," I hollered over the rain. We ran back to the boat as quickly as we could.

The wooden walkway became slippery. Rosie ran ahead of me but tripped on a jagged piece of wood. She flew and skidded across the walkway and slid off the side.

"Rosie!" I screamed.

She grabbed the side, dangling over the edge. My body exploded in fear and I ran over to her. When I reached her I grabbed her hands and pulled her up. The rain now came down even harder and Rosie started to slip from my grasp. "Hold on, cher."

"I am," she said, trying to hold on in the blinding rainstorm. As Rosie dangled above the swamp I used all my strength and slowly pulled her back up. When she landed in my arms I desperately wanted to kiss her, but we didn't have time.

"Let's get going before we are drenched and don't make it home. " I held onto her hand as we made it to the boat. We both jumped inside and I pulled the cord to the motor and pulled back.

All of a sudden Yvette turned and waved her hands in the air. This time as the rain came I concentrated and pushed the rain back at her. She flew backward, landing in the marshland. I felt an invisible barrier settle around us and glanced at Apris, but she looked as shocked as I did.

"Good job. I knew you could do it," Rosie beamed.

"Thanks, cher, for always believing in me." I kissed her.

She nodded. "Now let's get out of here."

The skiff purred and I steered us home.

Chapter Twenty-three

Rosie

W e entered the courtyard and were greeted by at least a dozen or so witches, who looked as if they had been in their own battle. I scanned the buildings around the courtyard, and at the top sat a stone gargoyle resembling the one I'd seen at Jahane's funeral.

I turned my attention from the gargoyle back to the destruction around me. Dammit, Gabby had been here. Stones from the walls littered the ground around the already broken fountain. The flowers had been uprooted and covered the ground. Our feet crunched on the broken glass and stone as we walked around the courtyard.

"Is Athena okay?"

I wondered aloud. Apris and Julian ran off to check on the other witches. Some were sporting injuries, and a crumpled body lay by the side of the wall. In a panic, I looked for Ares, but he was nowhere to be seen. Maybe he had gone to check on Athena.

My courtyard held a scene of utter chaos. Witches scurried around in panic. Two were hunched over the dead body, crying.

My head whipped back and forth furiously. What was I going to do? Was this my fault as well?

Elspeth walked over to me. "Yes, Athena is fine. Gabby never found her, though she searched for her in a tumultuous manner...as you can tell from the devastation."

"I must check on her."

I pulled from Elspeth's grasp. Before I could go and check on her, though, Alexander came out of the shop.

"Did you get the stuff?" His torn shirt showed off a well-defined chest. His red hair hung loosely over his eyes, and he brushed it out of his face.

Julian walked up to him. "We got the ingredients, though it was tough for a second or two." Julian handed him the brown paper bag in his hand.

We followed him inside the shop, where he dumped the contents onto the table. First, he pulled apart the red clover plants, blood flower, and a few others. He placed them in a marble square mortar, and then with the pestle ground them, along with the fresh sage leaves, into a powder. Afterward he poured the concoction into a beaker filled with some sort of multicolored liquid and swirled it.

"Amos...," he called out to the sentry.

"Yes, sire." He smiled and pulled the little brown pouch from his pocket.

"It doesn't hurt to have a little fairy dust, or as you say, a little lagniappe magic." Alexander poured it into the beaker. The sparkly contents slid inside, giving it a now sparkly effervescent appearance. Then he placed it over a small flame. "Now to heat it up. It will take a while to get to the right temperature." As the flame flickered the colors became vibrant, changing from pink to blue then to orange until the liquid had been all colors known to man.

I couldn't wait so I roamed outside, finally sitting in a rocking chair and gazing into space.

You know, Athena will be fine, a gruff voice spoke.

I turned around and saw the huge bluish gray dog sitting on his haunches.

"Um, did you just speak?"

He laughed in my head. *Do you think it is only Athena who can speak?*

"No, but I thought one would have to be bonded in order to hear a Guardian."

Yes, in retrospect one does, but I've learned so much in the long time I've been alive. Besides, I felt you needed reassurance.

Then a thought struck me. "Where is your witch?"

Sadly, he died a while ago. I've been living with Alexander and Alisa ever since Athena came to live with you.

"You have?"

Yes. When Alexander returned I was there waiting for him. He walked over to me and rubbed my leg with his head. *I chose to carry on my duties with another witch. I knew there was more out there for me. It was only done one other time.*

"By who?"

My mother. She wished to carry on and bring more Guardians into this world after her witch, Alexander's wife, died. We were both given a choice and knew that our destiny had not been fulfilled yet.

"Wait, you chose another witch?"

Before he could answer Julian came running out of the shop. "Rosie, we have the antidote."

The blue dog smiled similarly to Athena. *See, I told you. A minor setback, but she will be up and running soon,* the dog chuckled.

"Yes, you did. Are all Guardians smart?"

It's in our DNA.

I patted him on his head and followed the group to my room. My Guardian would soon be better, and then we could go after the evil trying to stop us.

Up in my room, Athena lay on her side on the bed. Her breathing had slowed and instant panic set in. "Oh no, we are too late."

"No, we aren't," Alexander spoke, pulling a needle out and inserting it into the bottle of clear sparkly liquid. It lit up the syringe much like the balls of lights the fairies bounced around in. He handed it to the doctor, and within a blink of an eye she had injected the solution into Athena's hip. I watched as the liquid moved under the skin.

"One more, Alexander. I need to get the next one into the blood stream."

Once again she stuck the needle into my dog, this time into a vein. As the liquid moved through her veins they lit them up and became sparkly, and then her body was a myriad of different colors, resembling the tear drop amulet around her neck.

All of a sudden the birthmark on my hip started to burn. I sat there in shock, holding my hand to my hip. The rose patterned birthmark on Athena glowed, and slowly the burning sensation on my hip dissipated.

Dr. Riella patted the dog and smiled at me. "Rosie, give her about an hour and she will wake, though she will be groggy. No food or water for the first twenty-four hours, no matter how much she begs."

"Thank you so much, Dr. Riella."

Her dark brown eyes twinkled and her lips turned up. "It was my pleasure, dear."

"Are you going back home now?"

She grinned. "No, actually, I've been asked to stay and help out the paranormal creatures in the city, since it's my specialty."

"Good. I'm glad you will be around."

"You get some rest now that Athena will be all right."

I turned to Alexander. "Thank you as well."

He leaned down and hugged me. "Rosie, I knew you were special, as I knew about Athena." They left, leaving me to crawl into the bed next to my Guardian.

I petted Athena for what seemed like hours. As I got up to go and stretch my legs, a voice stopped me. *Where are you going, Mom?*

"Athena!" I rushed back over to her and nestled my face into her fur. "Thank goodness you are alive and okay." I stopped and began checking her out. "You are okay?"

Yes Mom, just a little groggy.

"That's to be expected."

Then Ares strutted inside and Athena's tail thumped on the bed. *Hey, brother.* She didn't seem at all surprised to see him.

Hello, little one...though you are not little anymore, are you? he chuckled.

She grinned. *No, I'm not.*

"Wait, wait. Athena, you've been out...how did you know he was here?"

That damn dog actually laughed at my question. *Mom, we are both powerful; I sensed his presence here.*

The door cracked open and two small brown heads peeked around it. *Come on inside, Lil' Bit and Hos,* Ares called out to them.

One puppy hesitantly walked over to the bed, while the other one ran and skidded into Ares' back leg. He gripped the fur behind one of their necks and tossed one at a time onto the bed. They both rolled and hit a wall, as in Athena.

Sister.... Ares stopped, looked at me, and continued. *Rosie, this is the next generation of Guardians.*

Stunned, I asked. "Who are their witches?" But before he could answer me—if he would have—we were interrupted.

Julian opened the door to the room. "Rosie, come on, cher, we have a meeting of the covens. How's Athena doing?"

"She's much better."

He walked inside and glanced at Athena. "How ya doing, girl?"

She rolled over and cocked her head at him. I laughed. "She said she's doing better."

"Good. May I borrow Rosie for a bit? We need to discuss how to stop Henri and his evil band of rougaroux." He walked over to my Guardian and patted her on the head. "Glad to see you feeling better."

She turned to me. *Mom, tell him thanks, but he still owes me.*

I burst out laughing. "Damn, Julian. You still owe her, but she does say thank you."

"Hey, what about me getting the ingredients to save her?"

I glanced over at her. "Does that count?"

Maybe. She smirked and stretched out on the bed with the little pups curled up beside her.

"We'll be back. Ares, keep an eye on her." I walked out hand in hand with Julian.

Chapter Twenty-four

Julian

The sky began to darken as we exited. A crowd of witches had assembled. "What is this?" I asked. "I thought we were going to discuss Henri and his crew."

"We are, but...." Alma stopped. "We decided you need to hone your powers a little more, with Rosie's help, of course."

The girl my heart belonged to nudged my hip. "What do you say we get started?"

Rosie walked over and stood in the middle of the courtyard. She raised her hands in the air and the wind swirled around her, causing her dark hair to flow out. Before I could stop it, a chunk of the destroyed fountain flew at me.

"What the hell?"

She just grinned and chucked another piece at me. I dodged it just in time.

"No Julian, stop it with your mind," Alma screamed over the howling wind. "Again, Rosie."

This time dirt flew and covered me. I jumped out of the way but quickly diverted the dirt a smidge. Rosie smiled at me, her face lighting up as she did. The little minx was having too much fun.

She raised her arms higher and a piece of stone was flung at me. Concentrating this time, I stopped it but Rosie kept pushing it at me. I couldn't hold it much longer so I let it drop to smash down on the toes of my boots. Then I used my mind to crush it into dust.

"Julian," she screamed out, "you've got this."

This time she dropped her hands and the ground began to rumble. Each stone came loose from the ground one at a time and danced to and fro.

"Ah, cher, now you are just playing."

She nodded, her features heightened with the joy she was experiencing. "Now put them back where they belong," she instructed.

I emptied all thoughts and pushed one stone at a time back into the spots they had come from. But every time I did Rosie pulled up another one. Even though she had the wind blowing my body was sweating, either from exertion or exhaustion.

After the final stone was replaced, I dropped to the ground. Rosie ran over to me.

"Are you okay?"

I pulled her into my lap. "Cher, I'll be okay if you give me a break."

She smirked. "I can't."

"Why not?"

"Because Yvette and Gabby won't."

"By the way, how have you become so strong?" I asked.

She shrugged. "Don't know. I think I finally opened myself up to the possibilities."

"Hmm. Possibilities, huh?" I looked around at the crowd and whispered. "Then cher, give me all you've got." My lips curled upwards.

"Are you sure?"

"Of course." I stood and offered her my hand.

After I helped her up she stood back. The sky turned to shades of rich reds and yellows, the colors enhancing Rosie's features. My thoughts were interrupted for a split second by the beauty of this woman. Before I could stop her she raised her hands and tossed not only bricks but one of the iron benches in my direction.

As the bench and bricks flew at me something happened, something I felt come from inside me. An invisible force wrapped around me and shielded me from the bricks. Slowly the bench settled back down onto the ground and the bricks followed suit. As my shield disappeared Rosie ran over to me.

"How the hell did you do that?"

"I have no idea." I sat, shocked at my new power. Apris ran over to us.

"Just as I expected—"

"Wait...," I interrupted her. "What do you mean you expected this? How come you didn't give me a heads up? I could have protected Apris when we went to get the supplies for Athena's cure."

"You did."

"What do you mean?"

"I know you felt the barrier when y'all were back on the boat." She sat beside me. "Because your mother was telepathic."

"That was me?"

"Well, it wasn't me. I have to say a spell...you did it with your mind." I went to speak and she stopped me. "You needed to believe in yourself in order for your powers, all of them, to emerge. They have been hidden for so long by the curse."

Suddenly flapping wings turned my attention from Apris to something else.

"What?!"

"I mean you no harm. My name is Trinity."

"She's a gargoyle," Apris whispered as Rosie sat beside me. The winged creature walked towards us and folded her wings behind her.

"Yes, I'm a gargoyle. Maybe I can help you."

"How?" Rosie spoke up.

She crossed her arms over her chest and stared at us. "Just a word of warning. I see a struggle inside of you. Don't let your pain and the hurt of a lost loved one cloud your judgment."

Rosie looked confused. "How do you know I've lost someone?

"I saw you that day in the street."

A flash of memories came flooding back. "Who or what are you?" I stopped and thought. "I don't need you to tell me that. I think I am doing well with all the loss I've experienced."

She nodded. "I was once like you, but...." She looked away, sadness creeping across her face. "Now I'm different. I wasn't always like this. When my heart turned to stone, so did I. I was cursed."

"I'm not up to date on the gargoyle lore," Rosie apologized.

Trinity smiled kindly. "It's quite all right. Please remember, don't lose focus on the impending battle you'll have to fight."

"What impending battle?" Rosie asked.

But Trinity never answered. "I must get going. I should check in with Jasper." Without another word, she stalked off through the cast iron gate of the courtyard. It clanged and banged as she left.

⚜⚜⚜

"Ahem. We must get back to business now that it seems Julian has some kind of hold on his powers." Alma stood before us. The other coven members conversed on either side of the courtyard.

"I agree," one member spoke up. "What are we going to do about all the death that has plagued us since she came into her powers?" spat the witch as she pointed at Rosie.

I stood, almost knocking Rosie and the bench over. "This is not her fault," I said through clenched teeth. My fists balled up at the sides of my body.

Her face contorted, filled with rage and anger. "Oh no, it is because of her that my sister is dead."

"No, none of this is Rosie's fault," Alma said sternly. "But that does not matter. We need to rectify this situation. We need to kill the succubus."

The witch scoffed. "We thought you did that already. Yvette was supposed to be dead, yet she is still among the living. And she keeps killing, as does her daughter." She circled the covens, waving her arms madly.

Rosie sat back and sighed. I took her hand in mine. "Cher, none of this is your fault."

She nodded, probably not believing me.

"Okay, enough blame. Let's come up with a plan." I stood and dared the witch to defy me.

Everyone started talking at one time. Each person had their own idea of how to end Yvette's reign. I had my own, but kept it to myself, knowing Rosie would not approve.

"I say we attack when they least expect it," another said.

"Oh yeah, when will that be?" The witches started talking all at once and I grabbed Rosie.

"Let's go inside and get some rest. Let them finalize the plans. You've done more than your share today." She nodded, grabbed my hand, and followed me upstairs as the witches argued amongst themselves.

Later I woke to Rosie snoring softly. I scooted out of the bed, slipped some pants on, and kissed her on the back of the neck. My lips lingered on her soft neck for a few seconds more. Then I pulled back and crept silently outside via the french doors to the balcony.

Outside, below in the courtyard, stood Alexander and the huge blue dog. His hands were raised and I heard a slight chanting. I stopped in my tracks but then decided to head down. My feet slapped against the wooden steps. When I was on the last step Alexander turned and waved me over. I quietly walked over to him.

"Hello, Julian."

"Hello, Alexander. What are you doing here?" I stopped at my apparent tone of rudeness. "Sorry."

He smiled kindly. "Don't be sorry. I would ask the same thing of a stranger in my home." I waited for him to answer me. "It's a very simple reason. I came to place an extra barrier around the place."

"This late?"

He laughed. "Of course...this city never sleeps. I needed peace and quiet to perform the spell."

I looked up and saw the twinkling lights of the fairies in formation around the perimeter. "What about them?"

He chuckled. "This helps them as well. They need some sleep."

I glanced up and saw the fairies were actually curled up inside their balls of light. "I guess they do. Well, I'm sorry I interrupted you."

He shook his head. "No, it is quite all right. I just finished before you came down." Ares nudged my leg. "It looks as if he likes you."

I patted him. "You know, Athena hated me when she first met me."

"I heard from Ares. Said she called you a fleabag."

Laughing, I sat down on a bench. "Yes, I guess she had every right to call me that."

"Julian, don't worry, she trusts you now. She knows the truth."

"Yes, but she still likes to call me a fleabag."

Alexander grinned. "She has the sense of humor of her mother. Athena waited for years to be sent to Rosie."

I absentmindedly petted Ares as he shifted his head in my lap. "What's this guy's story?."

"His witch died of old age, and he chose to come back and live with me and wait for another to serve and protect."

"He can do that?"

"Yes, his mother did it when my Dahlia passed. She knew she had a bigger destiny. So does Ares." He patted my shoulder. "It's getting late...you should get back to Rosie."

I knew he was not saying something, but I yawned and stood. "'Night, Alexander."

"Goodnight, Julian."

I petted the dog one last time before ascending the steps. "'Night, Ares."

Chapter Twenty-five

Rosie

The next morning I woke and rolled over, patting the bed. My hand reached further across the bed, but I didn't feel Julian. I cracked one eye open and searched for him, but he wasn't there.

He's visiting his brother. Athena's voice made me jump.

"Geez, Athena, don't scare me like that."

Sorry, Mom. Thought you'd want to know. Not sure why he wanted to talk to that Mr. Creepy dude, though.

"How do you know where he went?"

Not sure. Had a feeling he was doing something he didn't want you to know about.

I rolled over on my back and looked at my Guardian. "Your powers must be growing again. And I'm sure he has a good excuse."

She nodded. *Well, if not our truce is over.*

"Hmm." I laughed. "You seem to be back to normal."

She licked her paw. *Yes, whatever that was helped. Though I plan on tearing that tattooed cretin apart next time I see her.*

"Not if I get to the tattooed bitch before you do," I laughed. I stopped suddenly, reminiscing about Jahane.

Mom, it's okay to miss her.

"I know, but we've got bigger fish to fry."

Yes, that we do.

Before I could speak again, a slight knock sounded on the door. "Come in."

A dark head peered around the door. "Ahh good, you are awake." Alisa sauntered inside.

"How can I help you?" I inquired.

"It's how I can help you. Well, Alexander and I."

"How will you do that?" I sat up in bed. "What do you mean?"

She sat in a chair beside me. "Have you wondered why the dogs are here?"

I nodded. "Yes."

"Rosie, I have visions, so I can show you what I see."

"Oh."

I watched as she removed a crystal ball from her blue and brown bag. She laid it on the floor and I watched white smoke swirl around in it. My focus was tuned to what I started to see, but then the door was flung open.

"Alisa, not yet." Alexander's voice boomed around the door.

"Why not?" she questioned.

From the corner of my eye, I kept watching the scene unfold in the round ball. Two people walked through City Park.

Alexander walked further inside, not paying an ounce of attention to me. "Because it's not time yet."

"When will it be time?"

"They must find out on their own."

"It doesn't hurt to push a little."

"Alisa, please."

As I tried to concentrate on the scene instead of the two people yelling at each other in my room, it disappeared. I glanced up and saw Alexander staring at me. He quickly returned his focus to Alisa.

"Fine." Angrily she stuffed the ball back inside her bag and stood. She crossed her arms over her chest and glared at him. "Do not to talk to me about time. Dammit, Alexander."

His expression showed a hint of laughter, but he quickly squashed it when she continued to glare. "Alisa, don't be mad," he begged her.

"No, Alexander." She stomped off.

He faced me and instantly his face turned a dark crimson shade. "I'm sorry, Rosie."

"No need to be sorry, Alexander."

"No, no, I should not be here in your room."

I laughed. "Oh, that."

He ducked out of the room, shutting the door behind him. I leaned back against the headboard and sighed. "I wonder what that was all about?"

Alexander comes from a different time, Mom.

"No, I meant the dog thing." I shook my head. "I'm so confused."

Alexander can be confusing and shut off at times. He means well, though, Athena said, getting more comfortable on the bed. She stretched across the foot and let her legs dangle off. I snuggled deeper down into the bed and contemplated what in the world Alisa had wanted to show me. But more importantly, why had Julian gone to see that traitor of a brother?

Chapter Twenty-six

Julian

Just before daylight I cracked open my eyes. Athena had at some time during the night crawled into bed. I scooted out and pulled on a pair of jeans. Sighing deeply, I brushed a hand through my hair. I needed answers to help Rosie find her parents' bodies, and I needed them now. As I thought how and who I would get them from, I made the decision to go and speak to the one person I didn't want to ever talk to again.

"Ugh," I groaned a little too loudly. Rosie stirred and I stilled in my tracks. Athena popped her head up. Quickly I placed a finger over my lips. "Shh. Tell Rosie I'll be back soon." I wasn't sure if she would relay the message to Rosie, but I swore that damn dog nodded her head at me. As I shook my head, I stood, grabbed my shirt, and pulled it over my head and pressed it against my chest and abs. Quietly I snuck out and headed to find the one person who knew where they were holding my brother.

My hand trailed down the railing, my brain taken over by an onslaught of thoughts. As I descended the stairs, Alma met me at the bottom. "Julian, where are you off to?"

"To speak to my brother. You wouldn't know where they are keeping him, would you?"

Her face showed no hint of knowledge. "Are you sure you want to do this?"

I nodded. "I would rather do it without Rosie to keep her safe."

"Don't you think she'll be mad at you?"

"Yes, probably, but I hope she'll understand why I had to."

"For your sake, I hope she does." At that, she grinned widely and hobbled off. "Hurry boy, follow me."

We walked down the cobblestone sidewalk. Alma tripped over an uneven stone but caught herself. She hurried on without even looking back at me. Down the street, we headed until we stood in front of the Ursuline Convent.

I gazed up at the façade. "Isn't this the old convent?"

"Yes," she nodded and headed inside the courtyard.

Trimmed green bushes lined the walkway to the façade of the French Colonial building. Even though it was a Catholic convent it gave off an eerie sensation. Once we had ascended the stairs I ran and opened the huge door for Alma. Upon entering the first thing that caught my eye was the hand-carved cypress staircase that wound around and up to the second floor. It was roped off, but that didn't stop Alma.

I put my hand on her shoulder to stop her. "Why is my brother being held in a convent?"

"Because it is the most protected place in New Orleans. This place has many secrets that most people are afraid of." As she said that something brushed against me and chilled me to the bone.

Before we ascended the steps one of the nuns shuffled out into the hallway. "Hello, Alma."

"Hello, Sister Agnes." Alma turned to face what now looked like an apparition.

"Are you here to see him?" she asked with disdain.

"Yes."

"Good. He's been behaving himself, unlike when he first came. Keep an eye out, he seems to be speaking with someone in there."

Alma gasped. "It's not a you know...?"

The sister laughed nervously. "You know, I haven't been up there to find out since...well, for a long time." She leaned in with her hands steepled. "That room is what can you say contained with evil." The nun eyed me.

Alma choked back another gasp. "This is Julian, his half-brother."

She held her gaze on me then scoffed. "I hope you are nothing like him."

"No ma'am."

"Well, I'll let you continue. Be sure to lock up and reset the alarm once you enter and leave. We don't want anyone getting out now, do we? We don't want the tourists to get one hell of a scare or.... Hmmm," she laughed, "that may not be a bad idea."

We continued to walk up the wooden steps through and down a secret passageway.

"Um, what did she mean by that cryptic message? And was she a ghost?"

Alma ignored me as we continued. She stopped just at the edge before the third floor, where she stood still and murmured something incoherent.

"Okay, hurry up the steps." I scooted past her as she turned and faced where we had come from and spoke something that sounded like Latin.

When she faced me I didn't budge. "Alma, where are we going?"

She walked past me. "To a place, no one that doesn't have a direct link to the Vatican can go."

"Then, uh...how can we go?"

She tilted her head at my question. "Because we have magic."

The vague answer had me shaking my head and chuckling. "Well, I guess that's reason enough."

A few steps further and down a hallway we stopped at a door. She pulled a skeleton key from her pocket and stuck it in the lock. It turned and the door swung open.

In the middle of the room, staring out the window that was boarded up, sat my brother. I walked into the room and a chill ran up my spine. Stopping in my tracks, I couldn't get it out of my mind that something was off in this room. "What is this room?"

But it wasn't Alma who spoke. "Brother, haven't you heard the stories of the famously haunted convent of New Orleans?" His voice was unrecognizable. He turned around and faced me. His hands were shackled and his wrists were bloody.

"What the fuck happened to you?" Not that I really cared. I was more curious about what or who had done this to him in a room that was so secure.

He lifted his hands. "You mean this?"

"Yes, that's exactly what I meant."

"Well, that's not really important, is it now? But what is important is your being here, Julian. So why are you here?"

Realizing he was not going to tell me, I spoke. "What do you know about Rosie, and what did you mean by wanting to help her?"

He laughed, and from the corner of my eye I saw movement. "I thought you didn't want my help."

"If it will help Rosie I am bigger than a petty rivalry. Besides, you can't tell me Henri treats you any better. Anything he touches turns dark."

"Oh, and being here is so much better than being with him." He glared at Alma. Then a hint of an odd expression crossed his face as he looked off into the distance. I followed his gaze but saw nothing. Even though I felt we were not alone, I turned my attention back to him.

He stood and nodded his head toward the bed pressed up against the wall. I walked over to the bed and sat. He kept glancing off, but I got his attention by clearing my throat. "Dammit, Dax, we don't have all day. Rosie is in danger, and I am afraid of your mother and sister."

"You are correct. They have plans for her."

"What are they?"

"That's not important."

I crossed my arms over my chest and glowered at him. "Then what the fuck is important?"

"What if I told you Rosie's dad never died?"

Alma gasped loudly, and when I looked over at her she was as pale as a ghost. She walked over to him. "Is this true?"

"I can't guarantee it, but I have my suspicions that dear Mother has been holding him, and may I add having her way with him." Alma looked sick at this new development. Dax laughed. "Well, it is what a succubus does, isn't it?"

He glanced once again off in the distance, but this time I couldn't stop myself. "Fuck Dax, what the hell do you keep looking at?"

"He's looking at me." A tall blonde woman walked out from the shadows, smiling eerily.

"Holy shit." I stepped backward.

"I won't hurt you, not unless you speak to him like that again. Then I may have to rip your head from your shoulders."

My head spun around and I looked at my brother. He smiled back at me creepily.

Quickly I turned back to the woman. "Damn, what are you?"

She laughed. "I am what your people call a casquette girl, or better known—"

"What?"

A loud gasp echoed from Alma sitting beside me. She stood so fast the air around me swirled. "We don't have time for answers. Come, Julian, we must be going." Alma shooed me out of the room. "Dax, be careful," she said as she looked around the door at the two before closing the door and locking it.

"Damn Alma, what the hell? You look as if you've seen a ghost, and I know first-hand they don't scare you."

"One problem at a time, Julian. Let's get home and let the others know what we found out."

I shook my head. "But we don't even know if he speaks the truth, or if it is, where her father is located."

"That's not what I meant."

"Then what did you mean?"

"Later, Julian," she said in a huff. She stopped. "I apologize, son. Don't worry, I have a plan and I must speak to Alisa once we get home."

We hurried down the steps. Alma reset the alarm again and we hurried outside the convent.

Chapter Twenty-seven

Rosie

I stood in the kitchen, waiting for my cup of coffee to be ready. The intoxicating aroma of chicory permeated my senses. "Ahh, I love the smell of fresh coffee. Don't you, Athena?" I tried hard to not worry about what was happening to Julian while meeting with his brother.

She padded in and stood behind me. *Um, Mom, I don't drink coffee.*

I dropped my head and sniffed in the aroma. "I know." About that time the door opened and in walked Julian and Alma. I dropped my mug, spilling the brown liquid. "Thank God you are back." I ran over to Julian.

"Cher, no worries."

"What the hell do you mean, no worries? You went to visit that traitor." I pulled back as he glanced over at Athena.

"How did you know?"

"Athena sensed it."

Don't blame me, fleabag, Athena spoke with her mouth full of kibble.

"Athena, you aren't allowed to eat for twenty-four hours."

She spit out the food. *Aww crap, I am going to die,* she said dramatically, falling over on her side.

I sighed. "Athena, no need to be dramatic." I turned back. "And you...don't you dare blame her."

He grinned and quickly changed the subject. "Would you like to know what I found out?"

I stepped back and placed my hands on my hips. "Yeah, sure."

"Um, you may want to have a seat," Alma spoke up and led me to the sofa.

Fear resonated inside me. "What is it?" Dozens of scenarios played around in my head. I sat, followed by her and Julian.

"Dear, it seems as if...oh, how do I say this?"

"Please just tell me."

She sighed deeply. Julian grabbed my hand and rubbed it. "Well, according to Dax, your father is still alive."

I gasped and pulled my hand from Julian's to cover my mouth with it. Then I grew angry and stood. "Please tell me you don't believe him; he's a liar. It's another trick to stop me from searching for their bodies."

"No. We aren't sure, but I think with Alisa's help we can figure out the truth."

I sat back down and held my anger close to me. "Then we should go get her."

"I'll go get her." Alma stood, and once the door closed behind her I looked at Julian.

"Do you believe him?"

"I don't know. He has to have an ulterior motive...I just haven't figured it out yet."

"Where is he?"

"Believe it or not, the Ursuline Convent."

"What?"

"Yes."

"Julian, have you heard the stories about that place?"

He shook his head. "No, but I do know it's haunted from what Alma told me."

"Julian, it's more than haunted."

"What do you mean?"

"That is one of the places that is notorious for our vampire lore." He looked at me, his eyes as wide as saucers. "In 1728, women from France arrived in New Orleans...the reason being there was a limited supply of the opposite sex here. As they exited the ship they had unique trousseaus in the shape of coffins, but because they looked so sickly rumors spread like the black plague. They were brought to their new home, under the care of the nuns, until their respective marriages could take place. But these women were not treated well, and the king of France demanded they return home. Afterward, the nuns carried those young girls' coffin-shaped luggage up to the third floor, where they were locked up tight. A short time later the nuns returned to the attic, to find an unanswerable scene."

Julian interrupted me. "What did they find?"

I laughed at his apparent fascination with my story. "Nothing." He looked shocked. "Yes, the chests were empty. Hence the idea of the vampires being brought over to the new world by way of these young women. In their fear, the nuns made sure nothing ever left the third floor or was able to get inside." I stopped and almost laughed at the expression on his face. "Damn Julian, with all you've learned about yourself and me, this can't be a surprise. Especially not in this city."

"No, it's not that."

"What is it then?"

"I think I met one of these so-called casquette girls."

"You did? Where?"

"With Dax...she was in the room."

I stopped and shuddered. "Wait...is your brother on the third floor?"

"Yes."

I shook my head. "I wonder why they put him there."

"Alma said because of what was in there, Yvette and Gabby would never dare try to enter."

"Well, yes, that is true. But your brother may not get out alive."

He laughed. "Do you really care?"

"Eh, not really. I would like to know if what he says about my father is true, though."

"I thought you said he was lying."

"I think he is, but if there is an inkling of truth I'd like to know."

Before we could finish Alma and Alisa walked in. The young woman carried a multicolored bag, the same one from the day she was going to tell me about the dogs. She smiled and sat on the floor in the middle of the room, then placed a shiny magical ball on the table.

Athena plodded over to it and gently touched it with her paw. *Mom, I saw you and Jahane for the first time in this ball.*

Alisa smiled. "Yes, she did."

"You can hear her?" Julian's quizzical look made me snicker, knowing he was probably the only one who couldn't hear her.

"Yes. It's faint now that she has bonded with you, but I can make out bits of her speech here and there." She glanced over at Alma, then returned her focus to the ball. "Anyway, let's get started." She waved her hands over the orb. "Show us the truth of what the evil one speaks of." A cloudiness covered the inside, and as I looked deeper I saw a figure sprawled on a bed. I leaned forward and peered closer. A woman, one very familiar to me now, stood before him, her hips gyrating and moving closer to his body.

"Oh, gawd no, hell no...I've seen enough."

"No Rosie. If that is indeed your father, we need to see where the bitch is keeping him."

I continued to look away. I didn't want to see the she-bitch having unwanted sex with my dad if it was even him. But my curiosity got the best of me and I turned back around to watch the magic swirling before me. The more I looked the more things would look familiar, then unfamiliar. It was as if Yvette was tampering with our magic.

Alisa stopped. "Dammit, I can't get a clear reading on his whereabouts." She leaned back and closed her eyes.

"Now what?" I asked.

"Let's focus on maybe finding your mother's body. From that, we can tell if Dax is telling the truth." She breathed deeply and gazed into the ball once again. It only took seconds for a picture to come in clearly.

I peered into the orb and blinked my eyes. "Is that...?"

"Yes, it appears that Yvette and Gabby have taken your mother's body to St Louis Cemetery number two," Alma said, wringing her hands.

"But why that one?"

"Maybe to confuse you, since you have ties to the other one."

I stood up quickly. "Then we must head over there. I have a sneaking suspicion her focus is on something else."

"I agree with you, child."

The five of us stood in front of the cemetery, the similar iron gates separating us from the inside home to the mausoleums. Julian walked over and the gate creaked open as he pulled, but it only budged so much. "Hurry, let's get inside before the cops come." He ushered Athena and the rest of us inside.

We stalked inside and the gate clanged shut, causing the three of us to jump. As a scream escaped I muffled the sound with my hand. I scanned the old cemetery, home to most of the dead of our city. From the scene in Alisa's magic orb, I knew which direction to go. After a few turns by some dilapidated tombs, I stood in front of a huge mausoleum. "I think this is it."

Athena bounded up to the marble tomb and nudged the iron gate. *Mom, it's locked, but I can fix that.* After Athena hit it with her paw the chains fell free and the gate swung open. *Come on, Mom.*

Julian grabbed my hand and walked me over. When I stepped inside the crypt, a chill rose and I shuddered. The further we went, the creepier I felt. The vault was huge but hadn't looked like it from the outside, which I was sure had to do with magic. Inside the middle of the huge vault sat two sarcophagi, the same we had seen in the bayou. I ran a hand over the hard marble. Julian let go of my hand and began to push the top off one. Marble scraped against marble as he tried to lift off the top.

"Damn it, Rosie. Come see."

"What is it?" I walked over and peered inside. "It's empty."

"The other one must be your mother."

"It has to be. Now where is my father?" I paced back and forth. I knew what I had to do, but I knew Julian was not going to be happy.

"I'll get the covens to come and remove the coffins, and take Magnolia to her resting place," Alma spoke.

The walk back home was quiet. I stopped right outside the cast iron fence leading to the courtyard to steady my emotions. I entered the house and anticipation filled my body. My body tingled with what I knew I must do. I turned to Julian. "Um...," I stuttered, "I think we need to go visit Dax."

"No!" Julian said defiantly.

I stood. "You will not tell me where I can or can't go. Besides, Athena will be going with us."

"Dammit," Julian muttered. "Fine, but let's wait till tomorrow."

"No, we are going now...the sooner the better."

"Rosie, I don't think that is wise," Alma said. "I think Dax has aligned himself with a vampire."

I turned and faced them, anger surfacing on my face and causing my body to shake. The house rumbled on its foundation. "I am tired of being told what to do. Now if you don't like it you can stay here, but Athena and I are going. And I am not afraid of what is in that room with Dax." I stalked to the door, grabbed my bag, and slammed it shut.

Chapter Twenty-eight

Julian

I watched as the door slammed and knew I had to follow her, but was stopped by Alma. "Wait. Let me call ahead and let Sister Agnes know y'all are coming."

"You aren't coming with us." Then I stopped. "Uh, how are you going to call a ghost?"

She shook her head. "No, I think it's best you go with her. I have many ways to contact a ghost." She scribbled something down on a piece of paper. "Here, you'll need this to get past the alarm."

I took the paper and headed outside. When I stepped out onto the balcony I called to Rosie. "Wait, I'm coming with you." She stopped and they turned around and waited for me. Hurriedly, I jogged down the steps two at a time. "Come on, cher." I grabbed her hand.

"Thank you." She smiled and squeezed my hand.

We walked down the street toward the convent. Once outside the gates, I stopped.

"Are you sure you want to do this?"

She nodded. "I need to see if he's lying."

"But it could be dangerous. After all, a vampire is up there with him."

She dropped my hand and stood firm. "I don't care who the hell is up there with him, but I will get to the bottom of this."

I smiled. "Yes, cher, I believe you will."

Athena bounded ahead of us. As we reached the wooden doors they opened and we followed the dog inside. Sister Agnes met us at the bottom of the steps. "Alma called and said you were on your way."

Athena padded up and sniffed the nun. Her nose went right through her. She showed disdain for the dog, and I held in a burst of laughter, knowing she'd be paying for her disrespect to the dog. "Why is this animal in here? More importantly, why is it sniffing me?"

I shook my head, knowing this would not go well. Quickly I intervened. "Sorry, Sister Agnes, but Rosie doesn't go anywhere without Athena."

She stuck her nose up in the air at the dog. "Make sure she behaves herself then. I will not tolerate the tearing up of the convent."

I stifled a laugh as I watched Rosie and Athena roll their eyes at each other. This was a time I wished I knew what those two discussed with each other. Oh, how nice it would be to be a fly on the wall.

I faced the nun. "I swear they will be the perfect visitors."

"Good. Make sure you reset the alarm." She floated off.

I nodded and led Rosie and Athena up the steps. Before we got to the third floor I stopped. Pulling out the paper from Alma, I read off the spell to deactivate the alarm system.

The place is here, the time is the hour.
Break the seal, with this power.
Allow us to enter without alarm.
To complete our task without harm.

When I felt I had said the spell correctly I placed my foot on the step, holding my breath, but was almost knocked back as Athena raced past me. I held onto the banister and looked at the dog.

Rosie patted me on the shoulder and grinned wide. "Come on, you know she is impatient."

I steadied myself and followed the two up the rest of the way. When we stood in front of the door that held my brother, I tried to sway Rosie one more time. "Are you sure you want to do this?"

"I have to. I need the truth." She placed her hand on the knob and turned.

As the door swung open a blur ran past us. My first instinct was fuck, which I actually said out loud. "What was that?"

"I think the creature they didn't want out." Worry spread across her face but quickly disappeared. "We'll deal with that later."

A voice interrupted us. "Come in, brother. She'll be back."

We entered. Athena walked around growling and sniffing in every corner of the room. Once she was finished she sat, continually growling at my brother. He sat facing the windows, whose shutters I now noticed were wide open, revealing the sun setting behind the buildings of the Quarter. He never once looked at us, never taking his eyes off the window. I wondered if the shutters were open, how come the vampire left when we opened the door? But my thoughts were stopped when Rosie walked around and stood in front of Dax, glaring at him.

Chapter Twenty-nine

Rosie

As I stood staring at someone who'd helped kidnap me, I squashed my anger down. I needed answers; if my dad was still alive I needed to know. "Dax—"

"I knew you'd come here," he interrupted me, his voice full of hatred. He never took his eyes off the window. I walked around and blocked his view. His face was one of pure evil.

"Is it true?"

"Do you want it to be?" He grinned devilishly.

He was toying with me and I wanted to get to the bottom of this. "Is it?" I asked again.

"What do I get if I tell you the truth?"

Julian stepped up beside me. "Dammit Dax, stop playing with her."

He turned around and looked through his brother. "Why, Julian? I'm not playing. I want to know what I get out of this if I tell her the truth." Before any of us could move Athena lunged at Dax, gripping him around the throat. As things escalated I spit out the spell I'd come up with on the walk here.

Now must the truth be told,
Lies to cease and secrets unfold.
Hearts to be open and words not slurred.
Now only the truth to be heard.

After I'd finished Athena looked over at me, her mouth still around his jugular, her canines digging into the flesh and causing blood to trail down. She let go but kept her front paws on his knees, daring him to move a muscle.

"Now I'll ask you one last time...is it true? Is my father still alive?"

"Yes."

That one word made my heart lurch forward. "Where is he?"

He shook his head. "I have no idea. Yvette never told me." It was strange he called his mother by her name, but I shrugged it off.

"Why not? Aren't you her chosen one?"

"I guess she never truly trusted me. Gabby was always her favorite." These last words he said with his voice laced with sadness. For a split second, I felt for him, but it faded.

"Could you find out?"

"Rosie, what are you doing?" Julian grabbed me and shook me. "I know what you are thinking."

"Let go of me. I need to find him...for my mother." I fought back the onslaught of tears.

"You can't trust Dax."

"I know, but how else can we find my father?"

Julian shook his head. "There has to be another way."

I glanced back at Dax. Athena remained in the same position. "What do you suggest then?" My tone was a little haughty. "I'm sorry."

"It's okay, cher, I know the stress you are under. But we mustn't take this lightly. Remember, he helped kidnap you. He's also a rougaroux."

"Yes, but so are you."

"Cher, you know I fight every day to quell that side of me. My brother doesn't have that luxury."

As Julian spouted off all the reasons we shouldn't do this, I kept only one thing front and center in my thoughts...my dad was alive. "What if I place a spell on him so that we can return him here afterward?" I cocked my head. "It might kill two birds with one stone. I mean, we did let out something that wasn't supposed to be let out. Maybe he can also find her."

Julian paced back and forth. "I don't like it, but what choice do we have?" He grabbed me by the shoulders and shook me. "Dammit Rosie, this is not a good idea."

"I know, but what can we do? I need to find him."

He pushed back from me. "You know he's not to be trusted."

Nodding my head, I pushed back tears, ones I refused to let surface. Determined to be strong in such times, I turned to Dax. "If I let you out, do you promise to get the information I need from your mom?"

He grinned maniacally at me. "I promise."

Mom, I don't believe him, Athena spoke in my head. *But if you think he can help us I'll back you up.*

"I don't trust him, but I have no other option. He's the only one who can get the information."

"If my mother hasn't told me yet, what makes you think she will trust me now to tell you?" Dax scoffed.

I leaned in close to his face. "I think you are a smart guy...you can figure it out." I pulled back from him and smirked. "I mean, if you want out of this prison you will."

He nodded and tapped his chin. His different colored eyes sparkled, almost devil-like. "I'll do it then."

"Good, but I need a spell."

I walked over to a nearby table and pulled out my spell book and pen from my bag. I dipped my pen into the dragon's blood ink. As I touched it to the pages it flowed against the vellum paper of my book. The red ink swirled and moved along as I wrote my spell out effortlessly. After a few minutes, I had the perfect spell. I stood and read from the book.

Never hidden always in sight.
No matter the place. No matter the fight.
Here or there, always to be found.
Always to be seen the spell is bound.

I looked up from the book and smiled, knowing MK would be so proud of me. Hell, I was proud of myself. Dax shook a little. For an instant, I felt bad for what I'd done, but not for too long. I nodded at Athena and she stepped back, releasing her hold on him.

Mom, we must keep a close eye on him.

"We will. But Yvette will never give him the information we need with us around. He must be set free and put out on his own."

Yes, but Mom, that mean penguin woman is going to be so mad.

"Athena, really, where do you come up with this stuff?"

She sat on her haunches, licking her paw. *Um, Mom, she is dressed like one. What in the world is that thing on her head?*

I shook my head. "We need to get out of here."

Julian dragged Dax up by the arm. "Let's get out of here before the ghost of Sister Agnes finds us taking the prisoner out."

What about the vampire? Athena asked.

"We'll worry about that after we find my dad. Besides, I've got a feeling she will find Dax herself."

"We must hurry and sneak him out," Julian said from over by the door. We scooted outside and crept down to the second floor.

We hurried downstairs, and as we stepped off the third floor to the second Julian turned around and pulled a piece of paper from his pocket. Nervousness covered him in a gleaming sheen of sweat. I placed my hand on his elbow.

"Don't be nervous. Read the spell for the alarm and let's get out of here." He leaned down and gave me a quick kiss.

"Damn it brother, stop making out. We don't have time."

I glared at Dax and Julian read the spell to reactivate.

The task is complete it worked like a charm.
Now that we leave reactivate the alarm.
Close the seal with the same power.
Now we leave from here in this hour.

We descended to the bottom and footsteps approached as we rounded the corner. I whispered to Julian. "Take him outside, I'll meet y'all down the street." Athena dragged Dax out by his wrist, knowing she was not being gentle and was drawing blood. They exited just as Sister Agnes came out from the hall.

"Are you done up there?"

"Yes, ma'am."

"Good then."

I continued to the front hall and opened the door. It creaked some and I felt a hand on my shoulder.

"We know you let it out."

My face fell. "How did you know?"

"We know these things. You must be careful and bring the creature back."

At that moment I wasn't sure she spoke of the vampire or Dax. After all, they were both creatures.

I backed up out the door. "Yes, ma'am, we will find it and bring it back." As the words left my mouth her face whitened, and I was convinced she'd not been talking about Julian's brother. And I'd failed the test and proved her suspicions were accurate.

"You let *it* out," she gasped, dragging the word *it* out. Her hand shook as she grasped her neck, then she did the sign of the cross. "You let the creature of the night out," she kept mouthing, and fear crossed her face as I closed the doors behind me.

I walked down the path and outside of the courtyard. The three were waiting down the street for me, Dax being careful not to move for fear of having his arm ripped off by the Great Dane. Blood trickled down his hand onto the ground.

"Athena, you might want to loosen that grip."

I glanced over to Julian. After a look and words back and forth, the dog let go.

We walked in silence for a few blocks, the whole time my thoughts on the fear on Sister Agnes's face. *Have we done something bad by letting the vampire out? But it was really not our fault. I mean, it was as if she'd been sitting in wait for the door to open.*

Dax bumped into me with his elbow. "Don't worry about Emilienne...I'll find her. She won't hurt anyone."

"She'd better not," I scoffed.

After a few more blocks we ended up back at home. Julian pushed Dax ahead of me and followed us up the steps. The front door opened and all the occupants sitting on the sofa turned their heads as we entered. Dax remained off to the side as we went inside.

Alma's face registered shock but instantly changed as she stood. "So you broke him out? Did anything else leave?"

Even as she asked we knew she already knew the answer, probably courtesy of Sister Agnes. I plastered on my best fake smile, but before I could speak Julian interrupted me and answered the first question only. "Yes...."

I pushed past Julian. "This was my doing. If you don't approve, please keep it to yourself." My brashness surprised me but I continued. "I needed him out so he could find the location of my father."

Alma tapped her chin. "So what he said was true?"

I nodded. "I put a truth spell on him."

"Well then, let's get down to business. What is the plan? You do have a plan, don't you?" She eyed me.

"We send him off to return to Mommy dearest and get the info I need."

"How do we make sure he comes back?"

I laughed almost eerily. "I've placed another spell on him so he has to return to us after he has found his location."

"Well then, if you feel confident that your spell will work let's get him out there." Alma nodded for Dax to leave.

My chest tightened as Dax opened the door and left. *Did I do the right thing?*

A soft voice echoed in my head. *Yes, Mom. Besides, I have confidence in your spells.*

"I appreciate that. I mean, after all, I have screwed up enough for multiple lifetimes."

Yes, but you are becoming confident in your powers. You proved it by not thinking and just doing. Besides, your magical spell book would have let you know if the spell was wrong.

I patted her head. "Thanks for always believing in me."

Julian came over and wrapped his arms around me and kissed me on the back of the neck. "I believe in you too, cher." Then I realized I'd been carrying on a conversation with Athena out loud in front of everyone else. "Cher, I do believe you are crazy talking to a dog and all." He laughed.

I punched him in the arm. "Shush. Besides, I think you may be jealous you can't talk to her."

He shook his head. "No, not jealous. But you may be a little off your rocker," he joked.

"Yeah, yeah, so you say." I laughed and stood on my toes to kiss his lips.

Afterward I settled down, nestling my body into the sofa. Alma and Alisa said their goodbyes. As the older woman left she leaned down and whispered, "I know you want to find the answers, and I feel Dax is not all that bad, though I still don't trust him one hundred percent."

"Neither do I, but you know I must find my father. I also want to put an end to Yvette and Gabby's evil."

"I just hope Dax doesn't get caught in the crossfire," Alma said.

"Honestly, Alma, Dax made his decision to be aligned with the whole lot of them."

"I know dear, I know," she said, patting my shoulder. The two women left without another word on my decision to let Dax go free.

When the door closed and I was alone with Julian and Athena, I sighed, but soon realized only Julian remained with me. "Where's Athena?"

"I think she followed Alma and Alisa, though I'm not sure."

My stomach began to ache. "Are you sure? I mean, what if something else happens to her."

He sat beside me, placing his hand on my knee, and patted. "Don't worry, she's smart," he leaned in closer, "and I heard from the whispers that Alexander made sure she would never be harmed again."

I sighed. "Oh, thank goodness."

"Cher, what's on your mind other than Athena?"

I looked off into space but spoke. "Do you think I made a mistake letting him out?"

"No, I think it was actually the only way to get the information. Yvette and Gabby sure won't give him the information with him being tailed. I think you did the only thing you could. Now don't go second guessing yourself."

"I won't. I promise."

I meant every word. It was time to believe in myself. After all, I knew in my heart that I had performed a spell that in fact would work and bring Dax back to us, with or without a word on my father's whereabouts. I snuggled into Julian's embrace and drifted off to sleep.

Chapter Thirty

Julian

Two days later

After Rosie and I had waited for any insight into the whereabouts of her father, Dax came storming through the door. He was beaten rather badly, but that wasn't even the shocker. Emilienne was with him, holding him up. His face looked as if it had come in to contact with a brick wall. One of his arms dangled loosely from the socket. The smell of fresh and old blood lingered in the air. His right eye was swollen shut, and dried blood caked underneath his nose.

"Athena, go get Alma for us."

Even though I couldn't speak to her she understood my command. She ran past the two and downstairs to the shop. Alma had been running the shop since we'd been back. Athena came running full steam ahead back into the house, followed by Alma.

"What's wrong?" she asked, out of breath.

"He's hurt," Emilienne answered, snarling at her and showing her fangs.

Alma stepped back a bit at the sight of the vampire but regained her composure. "How?"

"Yvette...," Dax choked out her name through swollen lips.

"That damn woman." She leaned down and felt Dax's head. "I'm sorry to speak ill of your mother, but she's pure evil."

He shook his head. "But she's still my mother."

"Yes, yes, boy, she is. Still, she does not have the right to hurt you like this."

Rosie stood apart from us, watching the scene unfold. Alma went to get some supplies to patch up my brother. He looked around until their eyes met. He inclined his head and she walked over to him.

Emilienne stopped her, placing a hand on her shoulder before she reached my brother. "This is your fault," she seethed.

"Get your hands off me," Rosie said in a growl. Athena stepped between the two, growling low, causing her hackles to rise.

"Um yeah, brother, call your bloodsucker off."

He looked over at me through one barely opened eye. "Lena, stop," he begged her.

The vampire released her focus on Rosie and stepped back. But the Guardian stayed planted firmly between the two females. At any flinch from the vampire, Athena growled. I gave props to the dog, being that she was catching the slight movements from the creature. I stayed close as well.

"Rosie, I was able to find the location of your father."

"What? Where—?" she gasped.

"All right, let's get him patched up." Alma interrupted us and came in holding a bizarre first aid box. She caught my look. "It's magical first aid, Julian."

"But...but...," Rosie stammered. I reached around and wrapped both arms around her. Dax's expression hinted at sadness as he glanced at Rosie.

"Now dear, he's no good to us if he goes into shock," Alma spoke behind me.

Rosie stood there and slumped her shoulders. Dax mouthed to her, "Sorry I couldn't get the information to you."

I pulled Rosie closer to me. "Let her heal him. Why don't we take a walk to the French Market?" Rosie's Guardian came up to us and sat on her haunches, looking up at me and blinking her eyes. I bent down to her level, which wasn't really too much of an effort. "Athena, can you stay here and keep an eye on Alma in her presence?" I nodded my head in Emilienne's direction.

The dog glanced at Rosie and they spoke their secret language. She swiped her paw at me, then trotted off to protect and serve. I turned to face Rosie, and she smiled at me.

"She said yes."

"I gathered as much," I chuckled, and grabbed her hand and led her outside.

Once outside, the air was cool and breezy. We walked down the cobblestone path to the entrance of the courtyard. The iron gates clanged as I opened them and escorted Rosie outside. After latching the hook on the gate, I turned to her. "So the French Market is it now?"

She nodded and her face glowed, a look I'd missed since all the devastating stuff began happening to her. The color flared in her cheeks once again, and it was as if for a brief moment she had stopped worrying, though I knew deep down she still did. Her small hand inside mine made me realize we could do this together, though it would be a long road. She was my family. We'd both lost so much, yet if my brother was telling the truth, she had to save her father from the evil clutches of Yvette. What in the world was she doing with him? Then I remembered she was a succubus, and I immediately shook my head at all the possibilities.

As we walked down to the market Rosie remained silent. "What's on your mind, cher?"

"Nothing really. I guess I'm just thinking about my father."

"What about him?"

"Do you think he's missed me? He's magical...I wonder why he never reached out to us."

"Maybe he couldn't. You know, to keep you and your mother out of danger."

She nodded off into space. "Perhaps."

I draped an arm around her shoulder. "Don't worry, cher. When we find him you can ask him all these questions. But I do know something; he'll be proud of the woman you are and the witch you've become."

She glanced up at me, her eyes glistening with tears, but the smile on her face spread from one ear to the other. "Thank you for telling me that."

Changing the subject quickly, I said, "What would you like to do before heading back to the chaos that is our lives now?"

"Anything as long as I'm with you."

Chapter Thirty-one

Rosie

After a long evening of shopping in the French Market, Julian's arms were laden with all my goodies as we walked back home. When we walked in, the room was quiet. In an instant I panicked, wondering where everyone was. Leaving Julian standing by the door with arms full of bags, I began searching for everyone.

"Athena?" I called. I swung the door open to my room and there she was, sprawled on the bed. She rolled over her jowls flopping, and popped one eye open.

What's wrong, Mom?

"Where is everyone?"

Down at the shop. Alma was getting tired of the bloodsucker whining, so she put her to work.

"What? She'll eat the customers."

Laughter followed me to the door, so I stopped. *Mom, she put a spell on her. The traitor is all patched up and Alma put him to work as well. I have to say her punishments are rather fun to watch,* she said, standing up on the bed and stepping off. *Come, let's go watch for a bit. Besides, she wants to talk to you about the plan.*

We came out to find Julian waiting by the door for us, a smile firmly planted on his face. He was having too much fun with this. "Come on, cher," he said, grinning.

Athena passed him and flung herself out the door, bounding down the steps to the shop. We followed, but I was in no way prepared for what I witnessed going on in my store.

As we went through the storage room Dax was mopping the floor. "What the hell?" Alma sat behind the counter helping a customer as Emilienne was straightening up the store. The bell above the door dinged and Emilienne looked up; her fangs popped out, but quickly her head flung sideways. I glanced in Alma's direction to see her hand was up as if she'd just performed a long distance slap to the vampire.

I made my way over to her, laughing. "What is going on?"

"Nothing, dear. Just teaching the bloodsucker some manners."

"Is it working?"

"Not sure, but it is quite fun," she said, smiling faintly. When all the customers had left, we sat down on the sofa.

"So what's the plan?"

Dax interrupted me. "Rosie, why don't we go speak to Henri?"

I spun around, knocking a few papers off the counter. Without looking at the papers I magically lifted them and placed them back on the counter. Then my hands went to choke Dax, but Julian came up behind me and held them beside me.

"Why would we do that? He hates us. In fact, it's his fault you and your brother are cursed."

"Because I hate my mother more. Look what she did to me...she used her magic against me. She doesn't love a single person. The reason the curse is on us is because Henri loved his wife."

"Still I don't trust him," I scoffed.

"And you shouldn't," Julian spoke, "but maybe we can coerce him to give us the information we need."

"How?" I asked, disbelieving.

The grin that crossed Dax's face sent chills along my spine. Then Emilienne walked up. "We have the perfect person to coerce or compel someone."

I contemplated this for a few seconds. "Do you think this could actually work?"

Julian leaned into me and spoke against my neck. "It couldn't hurt."

I shook my head. "I don't know. If we do this, I insist that we have a backup in case he stabs us in the back."

Alma walked over to us. "I agree," she said as she slid a plate of cookies in front of us.

"What is this?"

"Just eat one." She eyed the vampire as she reached for one. "Not you." Emilienne's hand flew back as if she'd been burned. Secretly I grinned as I took a bite. I knew Alma had done something to her. "Now eat." She leaned down and handed one to Athena, who had just come into the room. "Since you must bring her with you," she glanced in the direction of Emilienne, "this will protect you from any compulsion on her part."

"What about Henri?" I asked.

"Ah, the old man himself. Bring him an offering as you would the loa."

I laughed nervously. "What do you suggest?"

She pulled a bottle from under the counter. "Here."

When I glanced at the bottle, recognition hit me. "I've seen that before."

"I'm sure you have, it's Henri's favorite drink."

Julian spoke up. "Holy shit, is that named after us?"

Alma smiled. "Yes. How do you think Henri lives? He's got to get money somehow."

"So he distils rum?" Julian asked, shocked.

"Yes."

"So how is a bottle of Rougaroux rum supposed to help us with him?"

She grinned wide. "Trust me," she said, and then ushered us outside.

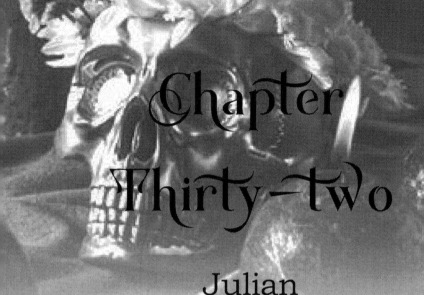

Chapter Thirty-two

Julian

Even though my gut told me this wasn't the best plan, I knew Rosie would go without me. "Come on, guys, we need to get going before it gets dark," I hollered at Dax and his whatever the hell she was.

Athena stood leaning against me and Rosie, growling when the two walked up to us. All of a sudden Rosie burst out laughing, but quickly covered her mouth and whispered to me.

"Athena is insistent that she sit in the back between the bloodsucker and the traitor. She wants to make sure they don't suck face." She stifled a laugh as she finished. I eyed Athena, and once Emilienne had scooted inside I nodded for the dog to follow.

"Dammit, brother. She's going to be a pain, isn't she?"

I nodded. "Yes, but that's better than her *causing* you pain; don't you agree?"

He scoffed, mumbled something incoherent, and slid inside. The huge Great Dane stepped into the car, making sure to press her paw into Dax's groin.

"Ow! Damn dog."

Athena turned toward him, her face inches from his, and growled, showing her canines. Saliva dripped onto his lap. Emilienne sat pressed up against the side because Athena's butt was pushing into her. She looked about ready to sink her teeth into the dog's hindquarters when Athena turned around and growled. She quickly rethought that idea. I laughed and closed the door after Rosie slid into the front seat. Damn, this was going to be one hell of a long drive.

After driving a good distance on the interstate we turned down a gravel road. The entire trip I kept glancing in the rearview mirror. Finally, after about forty-five minutes, Athena quit growling and sprawled herself across my brother and Emilienne, which, from the expressions on their faces, they were none too happy about. I pulled the Impala into the dirt drive, kicking up the rocks as I slowed to a stop.

"Careful, Julian."

"I'm trying, but—"

"Look," my brother spoke from his spot in the back seat.

We all glanced out the front window and saw someone walking out back, though the weird thing was she stepped down what seemed to be steps. She floated in the air and landed on the ground.

"What in the...?" I exclaimed.

"That's Syn."

"I've seen her," Rosie said.

"I'm sure you have," Dax retorted. "She's one of Henri's creations."

"What do you mean?" Rosie asked.

"He, uh—"

She interrupted him. "I don't care, really. Let's find out what is going on," Rosie said, opening the door and stepping outside. Athena quickly jumped out of the car, making sure to inflict pain upon my brother as she did.

"Shit!" he yelled.

Emilienne flew past us. "I'll take care of this."

We all ran after her, waving our hands. When we reached her, she had Syn in her grasp.

"Let her go, Emilienne," I snarled.

She flashed her fangs and let Syn slide back down to the ground, then focused her gaze on the creature. Syn wavered from side to side. "Tell us where you were coming from."

Syn stuttered and her tail whipped around her. "Uh, the secret house."

"What secret house?" Emilienne hissed out. "I don't see a house."

Syn turned around and looked back. "There's a house."

193

"Where?"

"Hold on, I think I can fix that." Rosie stepped forward and chanted.

In this time, in this hour.
I call upon the needed power.
Let the purpose be known.
Have the unseen be shown.
Hear me now hear my cries.
To let me see with newfound eyes.

Before our eyes, an old plantation house slowly came into view. The invisible steps Syn had walked down were now visible. Emilienne returned her focus to Syn. "What are you hiding in the house?"

"Yvette's prisoner."

Rosie wavered in her spot and grabbed onto my arm. I stepped forward. "Syn, do you know the name of the man being held, prisoner?" She nodded, fear registering in her expression. "What is it?" I prodded.

"Dominick Delacroix."

Rosie gasped and gripped my arm tighter. "It's true." I held her closer to me.

Chapter Thirty-three

Rosie

After the news, I plopped down on the wooden steps leading up to where my father resided. What the hell? So many questions ran rampant through my head, but none that I could utter. Athena sat beside me but never spoke. Tears welled up inside, followed by anger. When I blinked back the tears, the faces staring back at me were covered in mixed emotions. Not wanting to waste any more time, I stood and shuffled up the steps.

I turned to Syn and she smiled, still under the vampire's compulsion. Julian laced his fingers in mine as I wrapped my hand around the knob. As it turned I held my breath. The door swung open, hitting the wall. Sitting in a recliner in the room sat a tall man with his back to us, his dark hair peppered with gray.

"You back so soon, Syn?" He turned around and went pale.

Julian had to hold me up from collapsing. "Father, is it really you?" I asked, choking on my words.

He stood from the chair and walked over to me. "It can't be...I was told you were dead. You shouldn't have come inside. Where is your mother?" The questions came out in a hurry.

At the mention of my mother the onslaught of tears fell from my eyes. The man I didn't remember stood in front of me as the man I loved kept me close to him. I could tell he wanted to hug me, but Julian's protective hold on me stopped him. "Mom is dead."

He stumbled backward, falling into the chair he'd been sitting in. "How?"

Julian walked me over to another chair and helped me sit. He turned to my father. "We have many questions, as do you."

"First I want to know what happened to my wife."

"Mom was killed by the same person who imprisoned you here." He sat up and then dropped his head in his hands, his hair longer than I imagined for a father. He silently sobbed. I knelt down on the floor and grabbed his hands. "Father, how come you never left this place?"

He looked up at me through red eyes. "I couldn't."

"What do you mean?"

"Look around. Do you see any knobs on the doors or a way to open the windows?"

I glanced behind me. He was right, the doors had no knobs. Behind the sofa below the window was a broken table, the wood splintered into pieces. "Every day I've been here I try to break the window, with no luck. Everything in this house is impenetrable.

"How come you didn't leave when Syn came inside?" I looked over at the creature, who looked fearful.

"Because Syn never came inside...she only opened the door and slid my food inside."

"What the hell are you telling us?" Dax spoke up for the first time since coming inside the house.

My father looked at him and laughed. "Boy, you must be her son."

"How do you know?"

"You are the spitting image of her." He kept his focus locked on Dax. "Your mother is a master at her abilities. She cast a spell on this house to not allow anyone to be able to leave, ever."

Dax scoffed. "Old man, if my mother locked you up here it was to have her way with you, so she must have entered and left."

"Oh she did, but she was the only one who ever left. Like I said, she is a master."

"But Father, what about your magic?"

He turned back to face me. "I think she did something to hide my magic as well."

Athena started pawing at the door but it wouldn't budge. *Mom, how are we going to get out?*

"I've got an idea." Everyone in the house began to panic. "Quiet everyone. Let me come up with a spell."

The voices hushed as I sat on the floor, remembering all I'd learned since becoming a witch. I crossed my legs, dug deep inside myself, and pulled at the ground underneath me. The elements were mine to use. I pulled out my book and began to jot down words. They came to life as the dragon blood marked the vellum. I smiled after I'd written the spell. "Now, can y'all form a pentagram around me each person standing at the points.?" I faced the vampire. "Can you compel Syn to help us?"

She grinned and walked over to the shaking creature in the corner. Afterward Syn followed Emilienne and took her place.

Carefully I placed the book on the floor in front of me and raised my hands. Athena came and sat beside me to help me in getting us out of there. I placed my hands palm down on the floor.

The wood floor buckled and the windows rattled as I called on the elements.

Calling on the greatest powers.
Protect us now become ours.
Fire come to destroy and burn.

As my words came out heat erupted in the house. The flames crackled and shot up around me.

"Rosie, we will burn," the voices around me spoke.

"No, we won't; they are protecting us."
I continued.

Earth to grow over and let nature return.

The floor gave way to the grass and dirt underneath us as they sprouted up around us. The roof overhead shattered, revealing the old oak trees, and the Spanish moss hung in ringlets around us.

Water to rush, stir, and flow.
Wind to gust, howl, and blow.

Rain came down and the wind carried any remnants of the house away.

Spirit rise around us to shield.
The powers for destruction we wield.

As the last verse of my spell came out a calmness enveloped me. In the distance, I saw a figure resembling my mother. She quickly disappeared, making me think my imagination was playing tricks on me. I remained sitting as the earth, fire, water, and wind ceased to exist. The only remaining element, spirit, wrapped its protectiveness around us.

I looked around and saw the house no longer existed. Poor Syn cowered over in the corner by the tree that had taken its place. Athena and my father immediately rushed to her aid. The other five stayed in position.

From the corner of my eye, I watched as Yvette and Gabby came out of the other building. A strange feeling coursed through my body, electrifying every nerve ending. My fingertips pulsed, and I flipped my hands back, palms up. The veins underneath the skin turned colors, a shiny silver. I flexed my hands and smiled. This newfound power would not last long until I had my mother's body consecrated. But the spirit gave me this chance and one chance only. I stood as my two nemeses walked towards me.

Chapter Thirty-four

Julian

Rosie stood and lifted a few feet from the ground. Her body seemed to be filled with a strong power, one that took over completely. Yvette and Gabby stalked toward us, followed by Uncle Claude. This time I would handle him.

I eyed Dax, giving him the signal as we noticed other creatures exiting the house. Dax and Emilienne followed suit and we left, leaving Rosie to take care of Yvette. The bloodsucker stalked Gabby but she was quickly thrown aside, which I was sure did not go over well with the vampire. She stood as a creature went to attack her.

People flooded out of the run down shack and toward us. I used my newfound power and eviscerated two hooded figures that came at me. With my mind, I pulled their hearts from their bodies. They slumped to the ground beside their hearts that slowly stopped beating. Upon closer look at them, they appeared to be some sort of bad experiment gone wrong. One more came at me, and with the power of my mind I cracked each bone in his body, and I actually heard them crack in my head. I shook the eerie sensation off. The creature fell to the ground in agony. It only took seconds for him to stop screaming.

Blood poured and covered the ground. The copper smell wafted through the trees and hung on the Spanish moss. Death and evil surrounded us. I glanced over and witnessed Emilienne as she sank her teeth into one after another, and ripped the heads off others. Bodies dropped in her wake as she moved through the throngs of people. Her mouth and clothes were drenched in red. Dead bodies littered the ground.

I looked around for dear Uncle Claude and spotted him fighting with Dax. As I watched, before my eyes hair covered Dax's body.

I ran screaming. "No! Brother, he is mine." When I reached him I pushed him out of the way. His mismatched eyes turned crimson. A power surged through me and I blinked as my eyes watered, suspecting that they were turning red as well. "Don't do this, let me."

Uncle Claude growled at me. "I'd rather fight you anyway. Your brother has always been a pain in the ass the way he kisses Henri's ass." He faced my brother. "You know, you were never going to be number one in his eyes. He thought of you as a failure."

My brother lunged at him but I stopped him. "No Dax, let me do this." He backed off but glared at us.

My dear uncle charged me but I quickly raised my hand, knocking him to the ground. He jumped back up and growled, beginning to change. But before he could, I pushed him away with my thoughts and he flew into the air, falling against the wooden siding of the house. He slid down and from my spot, I saw his anger grow. He stood, continuing to change, the hair crawling over his body.

Before my eyes the monster I feared turning into stared at me. He stalked me, saliva dripping from his canines. I backed up but stopped quickly, my thighs bumping into something. I turned around and saw Athena. She nodded at me and smiled. But as I turned back to face the monster he came running at me and knocked me to the ground. His weight suffocated me.

"Why don't you remove that ring and fight me the only way that is fair?" he growled.

I shook my head. "No, this ring has more power than even you can imagine."

All of a sudden he flew off me and Dax stood there. "Looked like you needed some help. Besides, I'd like another crack at him." He offered his hand to me. When I was back upright we both looked back at Claude.

"You know, brother, this doesn't make me forgive you for kidnapping Rosie."

"I know, but we don't have time, we need to get rid of dear old uncle," he sneered.

Before we could attack, Emilienne came out of nowhere and sank her teeth into Claude. Blood poured and gushed from the wound. I glared at her as she dropped the body.

"Dammit, bloodsucker. He was mine," I growled.

As she clapped her hands she grinned evilly, blood covering her mouth. She wiped her mouth with the sleeve of her shirt. "Well, you two were boring the hell out of me with all this namby-pamby shit." I shook my head at her. Damn, I really hated her. She interrupted my thoughts. "Besides, I was hungry and the dog won't let me eat that Syn creature. But more importantly, I think you need to take a look at Rosie."

Chapter Thirty-five

Rosie

Anger enveloped me as I let the elements surround me and protect me. I raised up in the air, my body light as a feather. The air swirled and the rain pounded down.

Gabby ran to me with her hands raised. "No!" I yelled. "I'll take care of you after I'm done with your bitchy mom." As the words left my mouth, I raised one hand and she flung backward, skidding across the muddy ground.

Then I returned my focus to Yvette. Her long brown hair flew around her like in one of those cheesy horror flicks. The chilling grin on her face caused an involuntary shudder. "You ready for this?" I hollered over the roar of the rain and thunder.

"Yes." She squared her shoulders and pushed at me. I stumbled backward a bit but contained my stance.

I laughed. "Is that all you've got?"

"No, you little bitch. I'm going to do the same thing to you that I did to your mother."

This tactic I knew was supposed to catch me off guard and make me do something stupid. So I took a deep breath and vowed to not let her get to me.

She began to chant.

I call to the dark magic, hear me and rise.
Come forth and show your power to disbelieving eyes.
Power of the dark to me you must fly.
To do my bidding, because the witch must die.

As the words flew out of her mouth I stood still, balancing in the air. Dust flew around me and the tree branches wrapped around me, encasing me like a cocoon. They held me at bay, trying to suffocate me. But my magic inside bubbled to the surface and lit up my body; my arms began to glow like fire, and my hair swirled around me. The elements that burned inside were helping to protect me.

The trees slowly let go of their grip and waved in the gust of wind that I had invoked. I smiled. "Is that all you've got?" I calmly pushed my hands palms down, then raised them, bringing the earth up. The ground rumbled and shook. Deep divots grew in the soaked soil. Then I flung the earth at Yvette, knocking her off balance so she fell to the ground.

She stood up and dusted herself off. Her eerie smile chilled me to the bone as she flew at me in a rage. When she reached me she wrapped her hands around my throat and choked me. But as she did, my body turned hot and she quickly let go.

"Bitch, I'll get you for that."

I tsked. "Such language. Didn't your mother ever tell you it wasn't nice to curse? Maybe we should clean out your mouth with soap." I knew I shouldn't be taunting her, but I couldn't help it.

Her eyes lit up and turned black. The evil smile spread across her face. "No, but dear, I kissed your father with my mouth. I see what Magnolia saw in him." She licked her lips seductively.

In seconds I became vexed, but from the ground I heard Julian. "Don't let her get to you. Remember she's a succubus...she will use her powers. She's trying to goad you into making a mistake."

I nodded and refocused on Yvette, but it was too late. She waved her hand at me, sending me hurtling to the ground. I skidded a few feet, my body digging into the ground. A branch from the tree above me attacked me, causing scratches on my body.

Once I had contained the branch and threw it into the nearby marsh, I stood. Blood seeped into my eye and I wiped it away with the back of my hand. My body convulsed with anger and I hurled myself at Yvette, but she stood ready for my attack and flung me back towards the tree. My head bounced off the roots in the ground. I reached around and felt the wound. When I pulled back my hand it was covered in blood.

She stalked towards me. "You, little girl, are no match for me."

Before she reached me I felt a warmth surround me and turned to see Julian, his eyes closed as he concentrated. He shielded me from any further attack from Yvette.

My hand dug into the ground and it rumbled. The oak tree planted to the left shook in the earth. Its roots, emerging from underneath, pulled themselves up from their dirt enclosure, and when Yvette was close enough the branches grabbed her and held her high in the air. Her screams echoed around us, causing the birds in the remaining trees to shriek and caw as they lifted into the air. Even from my position on the ground I heard the bones in her body crack as the branches crushed her to death.

The tree let go of her and she plummeted to the ground in a heap of broken bones. Before my eyes, the ground opened up beneath her and swallowed her. The tree that I had uprooted settled back over the hole that contained Yvette.

I still heard screaming, but it came from Gabby, not her mother. The screams reverberated off the air around us. I let the elements settle back down to their respective places and leaned forward, sighing in relief.

Gabby came running at me, but before she reached me, Athena forcefully dragged her backward. The dog knocked her down and growled.

"Athena, back off...let her go for now."

But Mom, she whined.

I smiled. "Later." I turned to Gabby. "If I ever see you again I'll let Athena tear you to shreds."

She stood, but Athena gripped her arm and pulled. The snake tattoo came off her arm and hissed at her. My Guardian reacted and chomped at the snake, taking its head in her mouth. Blood spurted and Gabby screamed, "Asp," in agony. Athena spit out the snake head and bounded off with a smile on her face.

"You shouldn't have done that."

Yeah, I know, but I wanted to leave her with something.

"Well, that you did."

We watched as Gabby ran off to probably receive comfort from Henri.

Julian wrapped his arms around me, giving me the comfort I so desperately needed. "Cher, are you okay?" He checked me out from head to toe, his hands sifting through my hair.

"Ow."

"Oh, I am so sorry, cher." He leaned down and his tantalizing scent invade my senses, all of them. He leaned in further and touched a fingertip to my lip.

"You scared me out there, but that was amazing."

I smiled. "It was, wasn't it?"

My father came up. "Rosie, you remind me so much of your mother."

He looked at me and I wanted to hug him. I wanted so much. I wanted Mom to know he was still alive. I wanted him to have his powers back.

Julian nudged me. "Go ahead." How in the hell did he start sensing what I needed, and when?

I let go of Julian and went to my father, the man I hadn't seen since I was a baby. He had the same stature as Julian but was much bigger. He wrapped his arms around me and I fell into his embrace and became engulfed.

"Rosie, I have missed you and your mother."

"I know, Dad. I know." I looked up at him. "But we need to get your powers back."

Chapter Thirty-six

Julian

Dominick faced me and offered his hand. "Since we haven't been formally introduced, now's as good a time as any."

I chuckled. "I'm Julian, your daughter's boyfriend."

He gripped my hand and shook it firmly. "Well, I have a lot of catching up to do with my daughter, now don't I?"

"Yes, you do." I wrapped a protective arm around her.

"Julian, why don't you get her home? I'll follow you."

I looked around. "In what?"

"Don't worry, I'm sure there is an extra vehicle around here."

"Uh, sir, excuse me," a squeaky voice spoke. "There is an old pickup truck out by the road."

"Good. Want to show me where?

Syn shook her head. "I don't think Henri would approve."

Rosie stepped forward and took the creature's hand. "We aren't going to leave you here with him." She turned to her father. "Please, could you take Syn with you?"

He looked at the creature and smiled. "Sure thing."

The five of us got into my car and waited for Syn and Dominick to join us. I turned to Rosie, and she smiled. "Already on it."

She whipped out her phone and dialed. After she had made at least four phone calls, asking the covens to meet at the courtyard, she grabbed my hand. I squeezed it and relished the satisfaction...things were behind us. She nestled into the leather seat as Athena, Dax, and Emilienne sat quietly in the back seat.

"So, no one is going to talk about the huge elephant in the car?" Dax blurted.

Rosie laughed so loud it caused Athena to bark. "What elephant?" she asked.

"The one where you kicked my mother's ass."

She turned around and matter of factly said, "I'm not sorry about killing your mother."

"Oh dear," the bloodsucker snorted. "Not that elephant."

"Which one then?"

"The power one," she replied.

"Oh, that one. I asked the elements to help me."

Dax leaned forward, causing Athena to growl. "You know you should have killed my sister as well."

"I know. But wait...why aren't you mad I killed your mother?"

He leaned back against the seat. "Because she deserved it."

The rest of the drive back we sat in silence. We pulled up to the curb and Dominick followed. After we had all piled out of the car I took a deep sigh as Rosie's father walked up.

"You ready?"

He nodded his head. "As ready as I'll ever be."

Rosie looked up into the sky and my gaze followed. The bright moon shone down on us, lighting up the street and the courtyard in front of us.

The chatter coming from the quad met us at the cast iron fence. I opened the gate, and it squealed against its hinges. All eyes turned to us, and deafening silence fell among all the witches. "Is the succubus dead?" came the question in unison from the crowd.

Before I could answer a voice spoke. "Dominick!" The witches parted as Miss Alina walked toward us. "Is that really you?" She held a hand to her throat. "Maggie will be...." She stopped. "Oh, poor Magnolia," she said, barely above a whisper, as she continued toward us.

I stood to the side, holding Rosie close to me. Rosie's father met Miss Alina in the middle. "Thank you, Alina, for taking care of my family."

She smiled weakly, "My pleasure, Dom...they are my family too."

He nodded. "Do you think you can help me with a little issue?"

"What is that?" she asked.

"I seem to have lost my powers."

She nodded and turned to the others. We all walked up to the covens. "All right now." She wiped at her face. "Let's see how we can help Dom get his powers to work again."

Dominick stood in the middle of the cobblestone courtyard as instructed. Elspeth stepped up first. "Let's see if we can find where your powers went off to, huh." She glanced up to the sky and raised her hands up, and the sleeves of her cloak fell around her elbows.

Searching near and searching wide.
Spirits help us with what we seek to find.
Her sire's powers need to be found.
Allow them to be known and unbound.

"Nothing!" exclaimed Rosie in panic.

"No problem. I've got this." One of the witches from Julian's coven patted her on the shoulder. She winked at me then gazed upon the moon.

In this time and in this hour.
I draw for a father's true power.
Bring it close to make it clear.

We ask it now without any fear.
Powers that really need to be known.
I ask humbly now that they be shown.

Yet nothing.

Witch after witch came one by one to perform a spell or other trick. Madame Claudette sat over in the corner, laying her tarot cards out. As she flipped them over and over I could feel her frustration. All failed in their attempts.

"Julian, what are we going to do?" Rosie asked me.

"I don't know, cher, but don't give up hope."

As I held her tight I watched Athena trot over to him. The witches had all formed a circle close to the shop, probably trying to come up with a plan. From the corner of my eye, I saw the blue guardian watching his sister intently. A high pitched bark pulled my attention back to Athena.

"Julian, Athena has found something."

We made our way to the Guardian. She sniffed his arm up to his shoulder, then placed her paws on his back. He held his balance as the huge dog gently checked him out.

"Athena, down!" she exclaimed.

"It's okay," her father reassured her.

Athena balanced on her back paws on the ground with her front paws now on his shoulders, continuing to sniff his neck.

Rosie backed off and faced Athena. "Yes, Julian, she found something," she said in a tone I hadn't heard since we'd first met. It sounded like hope and joy.

215

The covens, including Madame Claudette, circled us. From the middle, Marie Laveau appeared out of nowhere. "Please step back and give us some room." They all stepped backward as Marie stepped behind Rosie's father. "Dominick, this is going to hurt...well, hell, a lot."

She touched the base of his neck. He flinched, then screamed in pain. "Please hurry," he said through clenched teeth.

"Just a little more." She pulled her hand back to reveal a tiny vial. It moved slowly from his skin, inching further and further out. After what felt like an eternity it dropped into her hand. Dominick dropped to his knees.

"What is it?" I asked.

The voodoo queen held out her hand, palm up, to show where the tiny vial sat. "Not sure. Let's find out." She closed her hand around the glass, and when she reopened it a small scroll sat on her palm.

"It's too small. We'll never be able to read it," Rosie said.

"Let's see if I can help with that." Apris walked over. She waved her hand over the vial in Marie Laveau's hand and the scroll grew right before our eyes. Rosie leaned forward and gently unrolled the parchment, the words becoming clearer.

She muttered under her breath. "That bitch."

"What is it?"

"A spell."

She handed me the scroll. For fear of what might happen if I read it out loud, I silently read the words.

Magic far and magic near.
Let these thoughts be strong and clear.
Powers that be powers that bind.
Make this magic unable to find.

I needed to get rid of this spell quickly. God forbid if it got into the wrong hands.

"Wait Julian." Apris passed her hand back over mine and returned the scroll to its previous size. Then I balled up my fist and squeezed hard. When I opened up my hand only ashes remained, and I dusted them off to the ground.

"Thanks." I glanced down at Dominick. Sweat covered his forehead, and from where I stood I felt his pain. And if I could feel it, I knew Rosie could as well. He sucked in a deep breath.

Rosie knelt down. "Father, are you okay?"

"Yes, Petal." He choked. "I'll be fine. I just need to get my energy back and my powers."

The witches from the covens encircled us. "I think we can rectify that since the spell to hide them is gone," Marron spoke up.

We moved away from Rosie's father and the circle closed around him. They chanted in unison....

What once was hidden can now return
His powers within to rise and burn.
Reclaimed and ready to use at will.
Fully restored his mastered skill.

As I held on to her I glanced down at Rosie. A painful expression crossed her face. "What is it, cher?"

"Nothing," she lied.

Her father emerged from the circle of witches and grabbed her shoulders. "What is it?"

She hiccupped. "Nothing. It's just that Mama used to call me Petal."

He chuckled. "Who do you think gave you that nickname?"

"You?" she asked softly.

He tilted her chin up. "You two were my beautiful flowers. When you were born you were so tiny, like a delicate petal. So I decided I would call you that. Your mom must have kept it up to keep a part of me around you."

Miss Alina walked up. "She did that. She wanted you to have a part of your father with you always."

Rosie fidgeted with the bracelet around her wrist. She leaned into me and whispered, "Julian I'm exhausted.

I patted her leg. "Hey, guys do you mind if Rosie and I get some rest? She's had a long day."

Dominick smiled. "I think that would be fine, son." Her father stood and hugged her tightly and whispered something inaudible.

Before we left Marie Laveau stopped us.

"Rosie, get some sleep. You deserve it. Tomorrow we will perform the ritual to consecrate your mother's body and pass her powers to you. Goodnight, mon piti." Then she disappeared.

Athena padded ahead of us. Ares stood at the top of the steps and seemed to speak to his sister. They both walked into the house.

"I wonder what that's all about?"

"Who knows?" Rosie said as she yawned.

"Let's get you to bed, cher." I scooped her up in my arms and carried her up the steps. Her body rested on mine, her head on my shoulder, and in seconds she fell asleep.

Chapter Thirty-seven

Rosie

I cracked an eye open as the light shone through the curtain. "Athena, close the drapes please." But my words fell on deaf ears. I rolled over and looked for my Guardian. Where was she?

I heard voices creeping down the hallway. Straining my ears, I heard an unfamiliar voice speak to Julian. I flopped on my back and then a thought struck me. "No, no, it was a dream."

Look who's awake! Athena bounded into the room and jumped into the bed. *Oh, and FYI, it wasn't a dream. Your dad is in the living room chatting with Julian.*

"He is?" I asked, astonished.

She licked her paw. *Yeah. I think he is trying to figure out if the fleabag is good for his little girl.*

"Geez, Athena."

What? It's true.

"Did you tell him about Julian?"

She licked the other paw. *Didn't have to, he sensed it.*

"He did?"

Yes, silly, he has his magic back, she said nonchalantly, as if I'd hit my head and could not remember the past twenty-four hours.

"What do you say we go see what they are talking about?"

She quit licking her paws and jumped off the bed. *Let's go.*

I scooted out of bed and my feet touched the hardwood floor, which chilled me. Hesitating for a second, I reached for Athena when she bounded over to me. *What's wrong, Mom?*

"What if in the morning light I'm not what he expected?"

Athena nudged me toward the door. *Please, anyone would be proud you were their daughter,* she said, continuing to push me toward the door.

I shuffled down the hall, and the voices grew louder. "So what are your intentions with my daughter?" my dad asked him.

"I love your daughter, sir."

I walked around the corner and stood quietly. My dad smiled up at me and changed the subject.

"Wanna catch a game sometime?"

"Sure thing, sir."

Julian saw me out of the corner of his eye and smiled. He turned to face me. "Morning, cher."

"Morning, you two," I said, smiling. "What's going on here?"

"Just getting to know each other."

A knock on the door interrupted us. Athena ran over and it swung open.

Alma walked in with Dax and Emilienne in tow. "Are you ready?"

"For what?" I asked.

"Oh dear, you have had a trying night. It's time we put your mom to rest. It's been forever. Hurry, Alexander and the others are waiting."

I nodded and shuffled back to my room. *Mom, I'll get breakfast,* Athena said to my retreating figure.

Once in my room, I sat on the bed. "Dammit." I fiddled with the bracelet on my wrist from Jahane.

I sensed him before he made a sound, but I kept my head down, allowing him to knock on the door frame of my room. Slowly I lifted my head to see my father standing in the doorway. "Petal, may I come in?"

"Yes."

He walked over and sat beside me. "Look, I have something for you."

"What?"

He pulled a gold item from his pocket. "This was...well, your mother and I had it made for you." The most beautiful locket sat in the palm of his hand.

I gasped. "How...I mean...where...?"

He laughed. "I had it hidden. When I returned I had Alina retrieve it for me."

"It's beautiful." I flipped it over and over in my hand, eyeing the intricate design. My fingers traced the beautiful mother of pearl rose trimmed in silver. More silver outlined the rose that sat on a red background. To finish off the design, mother of pearl outlined the round locket. My hands shook as I opened it. A photo of my mother when she was younger stared back at me. On the other side was one of my father.

"Would you like me to help you put it on?"

"Yes, please."

I went to remove the amulet given to me from Madame Claudette so long ago. He stopped me.

"No Rosie, you need both."

"But won't it be too much?"

"No, they will actually merge."

"Okay." I handed it back to him and lifted my hair, letting him clasp the locket around my neck. Once he finished I dropped my hair and felt the cold silver against my chest. When I looked down the two necklaces had merged together. If I looked at them I could see both as one. "Thanks, Dad."

He pulled me closer to him and hugged me. "Damn, Rosie, I'm so sorry for everything. I've missed out on so much."

For a second, as I snuggled into the chest of my father, I felt like a child again. His fatherly protection wrapped around me. "It's okay, Dad." I pulled back. "I need to get dressed. I don't think Mama would approve of me going to the cemetery in my pjs."

He chuckled. "Probably not. Okay, hurry up then." He stood and walked towards the door, but turned around. "That Julian, he's a good guy for being cursed."

I smiled. "Yes he is, Dad. Though don't tell Athena you said that. She thinks you are on her side. She denies that he is growing on her."

"Oh, that's just her Guardian nature," he said as he shut the door.

An hour later we all stood in the cemetery, my mother's marble sarcophagus held up by an invisible force. The witches, including Julian, formed a semi-circle around me and my mother's body. Athena leaned into me, keeping an ever vigilant protective shield around me.

"Are you ready, dear?" Miss Alina asked.

I nodded nervously. "Yes."

In unison, the witches began to speak.

Soul, heart, body, and mind.
A mother and daughter forever entwined.
Blood for her blood now and forever.
A link to each other that shall never sever.
Mother to daughter the powers flow through.
Generation to generation the power stays true.

The earth shook below me, but neither I nor the other witches moved. As I stood the fog settled in and crept eerily across the ground and covered the coffin. Off in the distance Baron Samedi stood leaning against a tomb. He tipped his top hat then puffed smoke into the air. Little skeletons danced to and fro.

My head swam with emotions, ones from my mother. A white shiny essence came out of the coffin. It danced along with the skeletons circling about. "Is that...?" Before I could finish, the essence slammed into me with such force it knocked me off my feet. I fell to the ground, my hands scraping on the cement. "I can't breathe," I sputtered.

Mom, it will be okay. It's almost over, I heard Athena say, but her voice was distant. As I bent over, a calming effect took place and spread throughout my body. First heat then a coolness flowed through every vein and bone and muscle. For a few minutes, I stayed slumped over and gasped for air.

Athena nudged my forehead. *Are you done? I'm hungry.*

Julian helped me up and kept his arm tightly around my waist. We watched the invisible force effortlessly slide the sarcophagus into the mausoleum.

Later, at home, we sat around the house. The rooms were filled to capacity with every witch in town.

A knock on the door echoed around us. The door swung open. Alexander and Alisa stood there, but quickly found themselves shoved out of the way. The two puppies ran through and around their legs. Alisa held onto Alexander before she toppled over. The whirling dervishes spun around on the floor, skidding on the slippery hardwood. The one with green eyes tried to stop, catching the wall with a thud to only bounce off and slide to a stop, sprawling with all four legs out.

I laughed and walked over to them. "Wow, they must be a handful."

"You have no idea," Alisa chuckled. Ares walked past me and scooped the puppy up in his mouth.

"Come on in," I said, ushering them inside.

Over in the corner, I saw Ares with Julian. Athena bounded up to me. *Mom, guess what? Ares has chosen to stay with the fleabag.*

I smiled. "Really?" I tapped my chin. "Well, I think he deserves to have a Guardian, don't you?"

Pfft. I guess so, but if he eats my brother he's in trouble.

I laughed and patted her on the head. "I love you, Athena. But he's not the one to worry about. We need to keep an eye on the bloodsucker, not the fleabag." I nodded in the direction of Dax and Emilienne. In a blink of an eye, they were gone.

"Well damn." I just didn't have time for this. Maybe I'd think about it tomorrow.

Epilogue

Julian

I headed over to the hotel where Rosie's father stayed until he could get an apartment in the city. A bout of nerves escalated as I knocked on the door.

He opened it. "Come on in, son."

I entered and stilled my nerves. "Hello, sir."

He grinned. "So what is it that you want to talk to me about?"

Hesitantly I started to speak. Brushing a hand through my hair, I took a deep breath. "Well, sir, I want to ask your permission for Rosie's hand in marriage."

His eyes went wide. "Son...." He walked and faced the window and gazed out. "Your mother was a wonderful woman, and may I add taught you manners. Though how can you be sure you won't hurt my daughter?"

Confusion took hold of me. "I would never hurt her."

"Are you sure?" He turned to face me. "You do hold the curse."

"I know, sir, but I am confident I can hold it at bay."

He nodded and said, "Then I give my blessing. But know that if you hurt her you will have to contend with me.

Three days later

We hadn't seen or heard from my brother and the bloodsucker for awhile. We just hoped for the best. Besides, if they didn't want to be found they wouldn't.

But I had other thoughts for tonight besides my brother. Tonight couldn't be a better night if I had created it, or better yet if Rosie had called on the elements for me. Above me, the fairies danced to and fro in their lighted orbs. Their movements in the night sky set just the right ambiance. Up above me sat a perfect full moon. I patted my pocket, where the one item sat that would connect Rosie and me forever. I'd prepared her favorite dinner with the help of Mr. Jacque. He had even offered to set everything up for me. In a quaint corner of the courtyard sat a table with two chairs, her favorite flowers in the middle of the table.

"Excuse me, Julian."

I turned around to face him and smiled. "Yes?"

"Are we ready to serve dinner?"

I grinned and looked around for Athena and Ares. They sat in the middle of the entryway, growling at the closed iron gate. "Hey you two, it's time."

Ares turned and nudged his sister. After they silently spoke to each other, they trotted over to me.

We are ready, aren't we, sis? Ares sat back on his haunches.

I leaned down and fixed something on Athena's collar. She craned her head as much as she could.

Is it secure? she asked.

I stumbled a bit at the sound of Athena's voice in my head. "Wha...?"

Ares laughed. *My sister is a quick study.*

After I'd regained my composure I looked at the blue merle, Great Dane.

Don't get used to it, fleabag. I just want to make sure my Rosie's surprise goes off without any mistakes.

A deep laugh escaped me. "Well then, it is secure, but if you want to make sure you can." I grinned.

Nah, I guess I trust you. She pranced off to her hiding spot.

I shook my head at her retreating form. *She likes you, don't worry*, Ares said as he followed her.

Rosie stepped outside and I became a nervous bundle. She glanced up and smiled at the dozen or so fairies dancing above our heads. I brushed a hand through my hair, then pulled out a handkerchief from my pocket to wipe the sweat from my forehead.

The girl of my dreams descended the steps, the red dress she wore causing my body to go into overdrive. It was the same dress from that night so long ago, the one where I talked her into going on a date with me. The flow of the dress as she walked towards me, the swell of her breasts as she breathed, made my breath catch in my throat.

"Hello, cher."

"Julian—"

I interrupted her with one finger caressing her lips. "You look beautiful."

"Thanks, but why did you have me get all dressed up?"

"I have a special surprise for you. Here sit." I pulled the chair out and she sat.

"What is it?" I knew to give her the surprise first before dinner, so I waved Athena over to the table. She padded out and headed over to us. "What...?"

She stopped speaking as her Guardian got closer. When she sat the rose lifted off her collar and floated in the air. Rosie gasped as it opened, revealing the diamond ring I planned to put on her finger. I plucked it from the air and knelt down on one knee.

"Cher, from the time I laid eyes on you that day by the amphitheater I knew you were the one for me. You've been my rock, my soulmate. Will you make me the happiest man alive and continue this wild ride we're on?"

Her eyes glistened with tears. But before she could speak a dark swirl of smoke wrapped around us.

"What the f...?"

"What a beautiful night it is tonight." A dark voice echoed through the air as we stood in the courtyard. Black smoke swirled around Rosie as she was separated from everyone. The same creature from the courtyard that day Athena had been poisoned revealed himself. He looked up to the sky. "It's a perfect full moon, don't you agree?" He sneered. "I've come for my offering. Rosie Delacroix, do you have it?"

She shook her head. "No, I don't. You need to go away."

He snarled, showing a toothless smile and black eyes. "I'm not leaving without what I came for," he demanded. "If you won't give me the dog I'll take you."

I stepped forward and spoke. "I offer myself."

Rosie turned around and screamed, "No! You can't."

Pulling her close to me as she struggled in my grasp, I said, "Cher, if I've learned anything from my time here, I've learned how much you give of yourself to those you love. It's my turn." I bent down and whispered in her ear, inhaling her scent of roses. She shivered as my hot breath pierced her skin. "If I know you, you'll do anything to save me. Please let me go and live your life.

"I can't without you."

She held firm to me. I knew as she wrapped her arms around me that she wouldn't quit until she rescued me, or at least died trying.

"Are you ready to go?" the demon asked.

Ares walked up to me. *You aren't going without me.*

The demon shook his head. "Ooh, two for the price of one."

I turned to Rosie and Athena. "I love you."

"No, don't leave me," she cried out.

As the demon grabbed me, the diamond ring fell from my hand. But my gaze never left Rosie as shock registered on her face. She looked to Athena then picked up the ring. A tear drop fell from her eye and fell to the open palm containing the diamond. She closed her fist around the ring. The ground opened up and Ares and I were engulfed.

To be continued…

Voodoo Vows
Magical Memories
Voodoo Vows Book 1
Ghosts from the Past Book
Black Magic Betrayal Book 2

The Guardians a Voodoo Vows Tail
Bred by Magic Book 1
Gifted by Magic Book 2

The Cresent City Sentries
Stone Hearts

Bayou Kiss Series
Summer's Kiss

A Legacy Falls Novella
An Unexpected Hero

Coming Soon
Trapped by Magic
Ghosts from the Present
Stone Player
Autum's Kiss
The Protector's Kiss
The Gryphon's Revenge
The Bear's Redemption

About the Author

As a young girl, Diana Marie Dubois was an avid reader and was often found in the local public library. Now you find her working in her local library. Hailing from the culture filled state of Louisiana, just outside of New Orleans; her biggest inspiration has always been the infamous Anne Rice and her tales of Vampires. It was those very stories that inspired Diana to take hold of her dreams and begin writing. She is now working on her first series, Voodoo Vows.

Amazon Page: http://www.amazon.com/-/e/B00O97TWUO

Facebook: https://www.facebook.com/diana.m.dubois

Goodreads
https://www.goodreads.com/author/show/7690662.Diana_Marie_DuBois

Instagram: http://instagram.com/dianamariedubois

Pintererst: http://www.pinterest.com/dianamdubois/

Twitter: https://twitter.com/DianaMDuBois

Tumblr: http://dianamariedubois.tumblr.com/

Website: www.dianamariedubois.com

Made in the USA
Columbia, SC
16 September 2022

67185676R00133